P9-DUS-257

Wifey's
NEXT
Deadly
HUSTLE

Also by Kiki Swinson

The Playing Dirty Series: *Playing Dirty, Notorious, Playing
With Fire, Playing Their Games*
The Candy Shop
A Sticky Situation
The Wifey Series: *Wifey, I'm Still Wifey, Life After Wifey,
Still Wifey Material*
Wife Extraordinaire Series: *Wife Extraordinaire* and
Wife Extraordinaire Returns
Cheaper to Keep Her Series: Books 1–5
The Score Series: *The Score* and *The Mark*
Dead on Arrival
The Black Market Series: *The Black Market, The Safe House,
Property of the State*
The Deadline
Public Enemy #1

ANTHOLOGIES
Sleeping with the Enemy (with Wahida Clark)
Heist and *Heist 2* (with De'nesha Diamond)
Lifestyles of the Rich and Shameless (with Noire)
A Gangster and a Gentleman (with De'nesha Diamond)
Most Wanted (with Nikki Turner)
Still Candy Shopping (with Amaleka McCall)
Fistful of Benjamins (with De'nesha Diamond)
Schemes and *Dirty Tricks* (with Saundra)
Bad Behavior (with Noire)

Published by Kensington Publishing Corp.

Wifey's
NEXT
Deadly
HUSTLE

Kiki
Swinson

DAFINA

www.kensingtonbooks.com

WITHDRAWN

DAFINA BOOKS are published by

Kensington Publishing Corp.
119 West 40th Street
New York, NY 10018

Copyright © 2022 by Kiki Swinson

To the extent that the image or images on the cover of this book depict a person or persons, such person or persons are merely models, and are not intended to portray any character or characters featured in the book.

This book is a work of fiction. Names, characters, businesses, organizations, places, events, and incidents either are the product of the author's imagination or are used fictitiously. Any resemblance to actual persons, living or dead, events, or locales is entirely coincidental.

All rights reserved. No part of this book may be reproduced in any form or by any means without the prior written consent of the Publisher, excepting brief quotes used in reviews.

All Kensington titles, imprints, and distributed lines are available at special quantity discounts for bulk purchases for sales promotion, premiums, fund-raising, and educational or institutional use.

Special book excerpts or customized printings can also be created to fit specific needs. For details, write or phone the office of the Kensington Sales Manager: Kensington Publishing Corp., 119 West 40th Street, New York, NY 10018. Attn. Sales Department. Phone: 1-800-221-2647.

The Dafina logo is a trademark of Kensington Publishing Corp.

ISBN: 978-1-4967-3476-1
First Trade Paperback Printing: September 2022

10 9 8 7 6 5 4 3 2 1

Printed in the United States of America

Chapter 1

Death Comes Easy

I can't believe how fast my life has turned upside down right before my very own eyes. I left Virginia to start a new life, but it seems like I'm cursed everywhere I go.

"Your boyfriend tried to kill your father," one of the cops said as he passed me.

Trying hard to digest what the cop had just said, I swallowed hard. But there was nothing in my mouth. Everything around me started spinning around in circles. I looked around the waiting room to see if I could see Dylan, but the cops had already taken him out of the hospital. Then I looked at Nick, who was sitting next to me. "That is a fucking lie! Dylan would never do that. You better check on those niggas in the streets. They've been trying to get at me and my father for the last couple of fucking weeks!" I screamed at the officer.

"Calm down, Kira. Be quiet," Nick whispered.

I stood my ground. "No! Fuck that! They don't know what they're talking about!" I shouted.

"Kira, it's true." Nick continued to whisper. "Your pops ran across the package of dope I left by the house. And when your pops confronted Dylan about it, they got into a heated altercation. And when your pops threatened to call the cops, Dylan shot him."

"Oh my God! Nick, please tell me this isn't true," I said.

"I'm sorry, sis. But this shit is real!"

A ball of emotions engulfed me. I immediately became dizzy while I wrapped my mind around Dylan shooting my father. I didn't know if I was coming or going. "What am I going to do now?"

"I don't know. But I gotta warn you about something."

"What is it?"

"Your pops is going to be a very wanted man after today."

"What do you mean?"

"The fact that he is in the hospital and talking to the cops is sending out a bad message."

"Who is he sending out the message to?"

"Kira, Dylan and I have a ton of niggas on the block working for us, but also bear in mind that we've got people that we answer to as well. In other words, it will be a good idea to go back there and talk to your pops and convince him to change his story because Dylan doesn't need that type of heat on him right now."

"But what if I can't get my father to cooperate?"

"Only Dylan could answer that," he said, and then fell silent.

Chapter 2

What the Fuck Just Happened

Did the cops just arrest Dylan for shooting my father? If not, please wake me up from this fucking nightmare because this shit can't be real. Dylan wouldn't dare do anything like that. He has too much to lose. Besides that, he knew how much my father meant to me, so these allegations have to be false.

"Nick, please tell me this isn't true," I begged him. He was only standing a few feet away from me, so I tugged at his arm.

"Come on. Let's go outside." He whispered to me and then he escorted me out of the emergency room through the sliding doors.

As we began to walk towards the parking lot of the hospital, Nick started laying everything out for me. "While you and I were gone to your pop's house to pick up his things, he started snooping around y'all crib while Dylan was in the bathroom. When he found the dope I had just dropped off to Dylan, he ran up on him after he walked out of the bathroom and started questioning him about what was he doing with that? And was he a drug dealer? So, Dylan snatched the package away from your pops and told him in so many words that he wasn't answering his questions and for him to mind his business. But your pops wasn't going for it. So, he told Dylan he was going downstairs to call the police. And when he started walking toward the front door, Dylan pulled out his gun and shot him."

Listening to Nick as he explained every detail of the altercation my father and Dylan had almost made me sick to my stomach. I stood there in awe. I honestly did not know what to do. But most importantly, I didn't have the slightest idea how I was going to deal with this situation. I knew one thing though: My plans to take my father to Hawaii were definitely out the window. How much more drama will I be able to handle? God, please give me the strength.

Tears started falling from my eyes at that very moment because taking sides between Dylan and my father was another issue I would have to face. "Nick, what am I going to do?" I began to cry.

Nick embraced me. "I don't know. But we'll figure it out," he assured me.

I stood there for a moment thinking about whether or not it would be in my best interest to go back into the hospital. Cops were swarming the place, and the last thing I wanted to do was answer a bunch of fucking questions about my man or my father. And then it hit me, so I turned my attention back to Nick. "What did Dylan do with the package?" I asked him.

"Don't worry. I brought it out of the apartment right after the paramedics came and grabbed your pops."

"Where is it now?"

"I've got it in the trunk of my car."

"Please get it away from here before the cops try to detain you or make up some fucking excuse to pull you in this bullshit," I whispered discreetly.

"Yeah, I thought about that. So, I'm gonna bounce. But call me as soon as you hear from Dylan."

"I will. So, keep your phone close to you. Because I'm gonna need the money and the number to that attorney you and he use to get him out of jail."

"I'm on it," Nick said, and then he raced off towards his car.

After I watched him leave the parking lot of the hospital, I walked back inside and eventually got permission to see my father. He was talking to Detective Grimes when I entered the room. Anxiety engulfed me at the sight of him because I knew that he was sucking my father dry for all the information he could. I wanted to turn around and leave, but I didn't because I feared that Detective Grimes would think that I had something to hide. So, I put on a brave face and joined him and my father.

My father spoke first. "Hi, baby," he said.

"Hi, Daddy," I replied, simultaneously leaning over and kissing him on his cheek.

"You remember Detective Grimes, right?" he asked as he pointed at the cop.

I casually looked at the cop and nodded yes. I changed the subject. "So, the doctor says that you're good and that you're gonna heal quickly."

He tried to crack a smile. "I don't know about quickly. But it's refreshing to hear," he commented.

I patted him on his leg. "There's nothing like good news," I replied, trying to make light of this situation.

"Ms. Wade, would you mind if I speak with you in the hallway?" Detective Grimes interjected.

"What do you want to speak with me about?" I asked him after I looked at him head-on.

"Well, for starters, I would like to talk to you about the drugs that your boyfriend deals in the streets."

"First of all, my boyfriend isn't a drug dealer."

"Tell 'im the truth, Kira," my father blurted out.

"Daddy, do me a favor and shut your mouth because you have no idea what you're talking about," I spat. And then I turned my attention towards Detective Grimes. "Aren't you a fucking homicide detective?" I hissed.

"Watch your mouth, young lady!" my father roared.

"You already have the answer to that question."

"Well then, tell me why are you so interested in whether or not my boyfriend sells drugs?"

"Because—" he began to say, but I cut him off in midsentence.

"Because nothing, stay in your lane," I replied sarcastically.

"Okay, well, let's talk about Nancy's murder."

"I'm sorry. But I don't have shit to say to you. Talk to my lawyer," I told him and began to walk towards the door.

"You do know that I could subpoena you to testify in front of a grand jury about her murder. And if you lie under oath, that's automatically a sentence of one year in jail?"

"Well, do what you have to do!" I yelled, and then I walked out of the room.

Chapter 3

Gotta Put a Plan In Motion

I couldn't believe how my father railroaded me in front of that fucking cop. This idiot has completely lost his damn mind. And for the life of me, I couldn't figure out why he did that. Detective Grimes made it perfectly clear that he wanted to talk to me even if it meant that I would do it involuntarily. To know that my father put me in this fucking predicament gave me a bad taste in my mouth. And if I couldn't get him to rethink this whole thing with him and Dylan, shit was going to get really ugly.

Immediately upon exiting the hospital, it dawned on me that I didn't have any transportation. My car was at home. So, I called a cab and had the driver take me back to my place. After I paid him, I walked inside the building and was approached by one of the building security guys. Mark was his name. He was an older black guy. He was cool as hell, and he often had conversations with Dylan about sports and life issues. So, when he stopped me to tell me that cops were ransacking my apartment, I became more furious by the second. "How long have they been up there?" I asked him.

"They've been up there since the paramedics carried your father out of here."

"Oh my God! I don't need this shit." I sighed heavily.

"So how is your father anyway?"

"He's fine. He's gonna recover real soon because the bullet traveled back out of his body."

"Well, how is Dylan? I've been hearing rumors that the cops took him into custody."

"Yeah, they did. So let me get upstairs to my apartment, so I can sort things out," I replied, and then I walked off.

"You do that," he encouraged me.

When I arrived on my floor, cops were everywhere. One of them stopped me right after I exited the elevator. "Do you live on this floor, ma'am?" the white female cop asked.

"Yes, I do," I replied and moved past her. But she grabbed ahold of the back of my shirt. "Which apartment is yours?" she asked me.

I snatched away from her. "I live right there," I replied sarcastically as I pointed towards the door of my apartment where all the cops were walking in and out.

"I'm sorry, but you can't go in there now," she told me.

"The devil is a liar," I said and stormed away from her.

"Lieutenant Smith, the owner of the apartment is coming your way!" she yelled.

"Yeah, I'm coming so get out of my damn way!" I yelled. I was irritated to the tenth power. How dare these cops try to keep me out of my damn apartment? I hadn't broken any laws.

A short but burly black male cop stormed towards me. "I'm sorry, ma'am, but we can't let you go in there right now," he announced as he extended his hands, blocking my path.

"But it's my apartment," I spat.

"I realize that, ma'am, but there was a crime committed here. So, we have to do a thorough investigation. And once that is done, then you can have access to your place again."

I wanted to smash his face in with my hand, but I quickly

snapped out of it when I heard a man's voice say, "Is there a problem?"

When I turned around, I saw Detective Grimes standing behind me flashing his badge at the lieutenant and me. My body filled up with anxiety at that very moment. I stood there frozen, trying to figure out what to do next.

"I'm just trying to keep the young lady out of her apartment until my officers are through gathering all the forensic evidence we need," the cop explained to Detective Grimes.

"How much longer are you guys gonna be?" Detective Grimes inquired.

"At least another thirty minutes."

"Okay. Well, just let us know when you guys are done," he told him, and then he turned his attention towards me. "Come with me so they can do their job," he said.

I got up the nerve to say, "What if I don't want to?"

"Come on, Ms. Wade, let's do the right thing," he insisted.

I hesitated for a second and then I stormed off towards the elevator. "Y'all motherfuckers better hurry up and get out of my damn apartment! And if you don't, then all of you will hear from my attorney!" I yelled, and then I pressed the button to activate the elevator.

Thankfully the elevator door opened only seconds after I pressed the button. And after I walked onto it, Detective Grimes raced onto it behind me. "Is there somewhere in this building we can go?" he asked me after the elevator door closed.

"Man, what do you want with me?" I huffed. I wasn't feeling him in my personal space, and I wanted him to know it.

"I want you to tell me what you know about Nancy Cox and the Mahoneys' murders."

"I don't know what you're talking about," I replied nonchalantly as I folded my arms underneath my breasts.

"Oh, you know something. And if you don't wise up and tell

me what you know, you're gonna be taken down, and I'm gonna personally make sure you get the maximum time for withholding evidence regarding those three vicious crimes."

"Do what you have to do because I don't have shit to say," I snapped. And as soon as the elevator door opened, I stepped off of it and stormed out of the front door of my building.

Detective Grimes stormed out behind me. He made sure I didn't get out of his sight. He caught up with me in the valet area in front of my building. I was standing there waiting for one of the valet guys to bring my car to me when he approached me. "Kira, there's no getting around this. You're gonna have to talk to me one way or another," he said.

"I told you I have nothing to say."

"Kira, let's face it. Your father told me everything. Now, if you don't corroborate his story, then I won't be able to help you when Kendrick and his boys come after you."

"Don't worry about me. I'm gonna be fine," I assured him as I looked away.

"What about Nancy Cox?"

"What about her?"

"So, you're gonna just let those thugs get away with her murder?"

"I don't know what you're talking about."

"So, you're telling me that you didn't see Kendrick and his boys put a bullet through her head?"

"Didn't I tell you to leave me alone?" I replied sarcastically. This guy was working on my last nerve.

"Kira, I'm trying to give you a chance to come clean. Because after I walk away from you this time, then there's not gonna be any room to negotiate. Absolutely nothing you tell me will help you after I walk away from you today. And before you say another word, think about how you'd feel if those punks would've killed your father. Now, wouldn't you want the witness to step up to the plate and help to get those thugs off the streets?"

I sighed heavily. "Are you done talking?" I couldn't believe that he was trying to play the game of reverse psychology. I'm hip to the good cop–bad cop bullshit! So, whatever you say to me isn't going to change my mind. I have to live out here in these streets. Not him, so he needs to back the fuck up.

"No, I am not. Do you know that I can help your boyfriend with the charges he's facing for shooting your father?"

"Look, man, just leave me alone before I blow up on your ass in front of all these people out here," I huffed. He had definitely made me reach my breaking point.

He stood alongside of me for another minute or two in silence. But after I gave him the evil eye, he backed away from me. "If this is the way you want it, then so be it," he commented, and then he walked off.

I watched him as he crossed over to the other side of the street. He didn't turn around once to look over his shoulder. If I was the old Kira, I'd have a nigga shoot him in the back of his head, and he wouldn't even see it coming.

Cops like him get underneath my skin. They always act like they're on your side and that they want what's best for you. But as soon as they suck you dry for all the information you can give them, they quickly throw you to the wolves without blinking twice. But that's not going to happen to me. I know what's best for me and it isn't snitching on Kendrick and his boys. If anything happens to Kendrick and his flunkies, it is going to be at the hands of Dylan and Nick. And that's just how it's going to be.

Chapter 4

Snitching Is Not an Option

I was a nervous fucking wreck after Detective Grimes left. I wanted to call Nick from my cell phone, but I was afraid to dial his number. The way things worked these days, it wouldn't shock me if my phone was tapped. So, I figured that the best way to communicate with him would be to take a ride over to his place to talk to him in person.

Immediately after the valet driver brought my car around, I jumped inside and sped off in the direction of Nick's apartment. Nick lived twenty miles away, so it didn't take me long to get there. His apartment was situated in a co-op style building like the apartment Dylan and I shared, but he lived on the second floor, and valet parking wasn't an option for the residents or the guests. So, after I parked my car in the garage, I had to contact him through his intercom system and have him buzz me in so I could have access to his building. "Nick, it's me, Kira," I said low enough so only he could hear me.

"Are you alone?" he asked me.

"Yes," I replied.

"A'ight, come on in," he told me, and then he buzzed me in. He met me at the elevator when the doors opened on the second floor. I was so happy to see him that I rushed into his arms. "Nick, I am so scared," I whispered into his ear.

"Don't be. Because I'm gonna take care of you until Dylan gets out."

"That homicide detective named Grimes is trying to get me to snitch."

Nick pulled me back away from him and looked me straight in the eyes. "What did he say?" he whispered.

"I'll tell you as soon as we get inside of your apartment," I told him.

Without any hesitation, Nick grabbed my right hand and escorted me down the hallway and into his apartment. Immediately after he closed the front door and locked it, he sat me down on a light gray leather sectional in the family room and started grilling me. "Where did you see him?" he asked me.

"First I saw him standing next to my father's hospital bed. And then when I left the hospital, he showed up at my fucking apartment."

"What did he say?"

"First of all, you know my dad told him that Dylan shot him."

"Yeah," Nick agreed.

"Well, my father also told him that we were there when the chick from my job, named Nancy, was shot and killed."

"Man, you gotta be kidding."

"No, Nick, I am not lying."

"So, what did you say?"

"I told him I didn't know what the fuck my father was talking about and I left. But I guess that wasn't good enough, because he followed me back to my apartment and questioned me again. I mean, he literally followed me up to my floor, and when the cops wouldn't allow me to go back into my apartment, I went back down to the first floor, and he followed me down there too. I had to get nasty and tell him to leave me the fuck alone before he got the picture. But before he left, he told me that if I didn't give him the information he needed at that moment, it would be my last window of opportunity and that when he comes back and locks me up, he's not gonna help me in any way."

"And what did you say?"

"I basically told him to go and fuck himself," I told him. I knew I didn't actually say those words, but he got the picture.

"Yo, Kira, we gotta come up with a plan. Knowing that that cop is sweating you like that isn't sitting right with me."

"How do you think I feel? This fucking asshole is literally harassing me. It seems like every time I look up, he's popping up out of the blue. And then he tries to intimidate me with all these fucking questions like he's trying to trip me up or something."

"You might wanna call Dylan's attorney for yourself. He'll shut that cop down from asking you any more questions," Nick assured me.

"Have you spoken to him yet?"

"No. But I left his secretary a message and told her that it was urgent. So, I'm sure he'll be calling me back real soon."

"Has Dylan tried to call you yet?"

"No. The cops are probably still processing him. I figure he'll probably go in front of a magistrate in the next hour or so. And normally when niggas get a bond, the cops will let them use the phone to call a bondsman or their attorney."

I let out a long sigh. "I hope so because I am on fucking pins and needles right now. Between that cop and my father, it feels like I'm gonna have a nervous breakdown."

"Listen, baby girl, just chill out and let me handle things. Everything is going to be all right," he said in a very sincere manner.

I wanted to believe him. But I couldn't. I was knee-deep in everything from telling Kendrick where Judge Mahoney lived,

Nancy's murder, and I knew about Dylan's drug dealings. So, how was Nick going to shield me from Kendrick or the cops? Especially since Dylan wasn't around to have his back. I know one thing: Whatever happens with me, I'm going to have to deal with it head-on. And try my best to stay alive in the end.

After Nick and I talked about the situation concerning Detective Grimes, his cell phone rang. My heart jumped into the pit of my stomach. "Is it Dylan?" I asked anxiously.

Nick looked down at his phone. "Nah. It's one of my homeboys that runs one of me and Dylan's trap houses," he told me, and then he stood up and left the room. It was apparent that he didn't want me to hear his conversation, so I was cool with that. Dylan has always done the same thing when he receives phone calls from the cats that work for him. He has kept his street hustle away from me as long as we've been together and I respect him for that. I guess Nick values Dylan's respect for me and has decided to pay it forward.

Chapter 5

When Shit Gets Complicated

While Nick was on his cell phone talking to one of his street dealers, my cell phone started ringing. My heart started beating uncontrollably. I looked down at the caller ID and saw that the call was coming from a blocked number. I was hesitant to answer it. But I had a strong feeling in the pit of my stomach that the call could be coming from Dylan, so at the last minute I answered it. "Hello," I said, my voice barely audible for fear that it might be someone other than Dylan calling me.

"Kira, honey, where are you?" I heard my father ask.

Hearing my father's voice made my skin crawl. I mean, what would possess this motherfucker to call me? He'd already got Detective Grimes breathing down my neck and got my man locked up. Was he on fucking drugs or something? I swear if I don't nip this shit in the bud with him, he's going to send me to an early grave. I sucked my teeth. "What do you want with me?" I hissed.

"Detective Grimes told me that you're not on board with us. So, I'm a little concerned about that," he replied.

"Daddy, I'm not gonna talk to you about this right now. This is not a good time," I replied sarcastically.

"Well, when will it be a good time, Kira? You've been dodging this issue since you told me that that drug-dealing thug Kendrick was the one behind Judge Mahoney's and his wife's murder." He was getting angrier after every word he uttered from his mouth.

"I didn't tell you no such thing, Daddy," I snapped. I was lying, but I couldn't admit that I told him that. This crazy-ass man could have the cops recording our conversation. That's how fucking loony he had become.

"So, now you're lying to me?" he replied calmly. But that only meant that he was disappointed with me.

"Daddy, I told you that I'm not gonna do this with you right now," I said once more.

"I'll tell you what. If you don't get on board with me concerning my friends' murders, then I'm gonna make sure your boyfriend gets nailed in court for almost killing me. And I'm gonna testify that I saw the drugs he had hidden in you guys' apartment."

Listening to my father threatening me about how he's gonna make sure Dylan gets a long prison sentence for shooting him, and testifying that he saw drugs in my house, sent my blood pressure up to new heights. I couldn't believe that he was saying all of this bullshit over the phone. Now my first reaction was to curse his ass out and tell him that he's dead to me. But then I figured that if I told him how I felt, he'd sell me out to the cops for sure.

My father was a man who was a law-abiding citizen to the core. I don't think the man has ever had a fucking traffic ticket. That's how much he took the law seriously. So, I knew that I had to play him at his game just to make my life run a little smoother until I could get Dylan out of this mess.

"Look, Daddy, I've got a lot of stuff on my mind right now. So let me get some rest tonight, and I'll come by the hospital and talk to you tomorrow," I finally told him.

"So, you're telling me that you're gonna do the right thing?" He pressed the issue.

"It means that you and I are going to lay everything out on the table and decide what would be the best course of action for it."

"Okay. Sounds good. So, then I'll see you tomorrow," he said.

"See you tomorrow," I repeated, and then I disconnected our call.

I didn't know until I had ended my phone call with my father that Nick was standing across the room from me listening to my entire conversation. He had a blank look on his face. It was a look I couldn't read. "Are you okay?" I asked him.

"I was about to ask you the same question," he replied.

I laid my cell phone down on the sofa next to me and buried my face in my hands. I held my face in my hands for a few seconds, and then I lifted my head back up. By this time, Nick had taken a seat back on the couch. "What was your pops talking about this time?" he asked.

"He still wants me to come on board with him and tell the cops what I know about the guys that killed his judge friend and his wife. And then he said that if I didn't, he was going to make sure Dylan gets nailed in the coffin when he goes to court for the malicious wounding charge."

"Wow! Your pops is bugging out like that?"

"Well, that's not it. This fucking nut case also says that he's gonna also testify to finding the drugs in my house."

"Yo, I don't mean any harm, but your pops is doing a very dangerous thing. Does he not know that Dylan isn't the only one tied to those drugs he found at your crib? There's a lot of people on our line. I'm talking about the cats we get our dope from. He could start an ugly war. And a lot of people would lose their lives too. So, I will be the first to say that if he weren't your father, I would get rid of him right now because I'm not trying to go into hiding so I can stay alive. No way. I've got too much shit to do and too much money to make. And I'm sure everyone else in my crew feels the same way. So, I'm gonna need you to handle this situation immediately."

"What am I supposed to do?" I whined as I buried my face back in the palms of my hands. This issue with my father was driving me fucking crazy. So what was I supposed to do?

"You're gonna need to talk to Dylan about that," Nick answered.

"But how can I do that when he's in jail?"

"Let's just hope that the magistrate downtown hurries up and gives him a bond so we can get him out of there. And from there, you both can figure out what to do because shit is getting ready to get real. And the way I see it, your pops may try to make you choose between him and Dylan."

Before I could utter another word, my cell phone rang again. This time the phone number appeared on the caller ID, and the words over it read: *Miami-Dade County Jail.* I was so freaking excited that Dylan was finally able to use the phone to call me. "Hello," I said anxiously.

"Hey, baby, where are you?"

"I'm at Nick's house. I just got here about ten minutes ago, why?"

"Put Nick on the phone," he instructed me.

"He wants to speak with you," I told Nick and held the phone out for him to grab.

After he took the cell phone from my hand, he briefly spoke to Dylan telling him to hang up and call his cell phone, and then he disconnected their call. "So, he's gonna call your cell phone?" I asked him. I wanted to make sure I heard what I heard.

"Yeah, he's gonna call me right back," he assured me.

A second or two later Nick's cell phone started ringing. He answered it on the first ring. "Hello," he said, and then he paused.

"Yo, Nick, put me on speaker so Kira can hear me," I heard Dylan yell from the other end of the phone. I also heard a lot of noise in the background, so I'm assuming that's why he was yelling in the first place.

Nick said okay, and then he pressed the speakerphone button on his cell phone. "You're on speaker now," he told Dylan.

I spoke up. "Can you hear us, baby?"

"Yeah, I can hear y'all. So, let me tell y'all what's going on."

"Okay. We're listening," I said.

"Well, it looks like I'm gonna be in this shithole until I go before a judge in the morning."

"What do you mean you can't get out until you see a judge in the morning?" I whined.

"Yeah, man, what did the magistrate say?" Nick interjected.

"First of all, the magistrate was a fucking bitch! So after the cops told her that I shot a retired judge, she took a long look at me and told me that she wasn't giving me shit and that I was going to spend the night in jail and go before a judge in the morning. But I know she's setting me up for another letdown. It wouldn't surprise me if she wrote something in my file telling the judge that I'm going in front of tomorrow not to give me a bond."

"Don't be so negative. Everything is gonna work out because we're gonna have your attorney front and center as soon as court starts," I told him.

"Did he say that he was going to come and see me before I go in front of the judge?" Dylan wanted to know.

"Well, we haven't talked to him yet. I left him a message with his secretary. So, he should be calling me back at any moment," Nick said.

"If he doesn't call y'all back within the next hour, then you call him again. Call his ass every thirty minutes if you have to. I can't afford to go in front of that judge tomorrow without him."

"Don't worry, baby. Me and Nick got everything covered," I assured him.

"Good. That's what I like to hear. But listen, I don't want my mama or my sister to know that I got locked up."

"Okay. I won't say anything."

"Kira, you gotta promise me. Because you know I know how close you and my sister are."

"Dylan, I promise I won't say a word."

"A'ight," he said, and then he changed the subject. "Have you talked to your father yet?"

I hesitated for a second for fear that I might say the wrong thing. I didn't want to make Dylan any madder than he already was, so I told him what he wanted to hear. Besides that, I couldn't tell him what was going on because I knew that calls from jails were always recorded. So, I did the next best thing, and that was to tell him that I had everything under control. "Yes, I talked to him. And everything is going to be fine," I lied.

"Yeah, a'ight. Well, handle it then. And I wanna see you at court with the lawyer tomorrow morning."

"Don't worry. I will be there."

"Have you been back to the house?"

"Yeah, but it's a fucking mess. There's stuff all over the place. I'm gonna call the housekeeper in the morning and have her come by and clean everything up before you get out tomorrow."

"A'ight. Well, handle your business, and I'll see y'all in the morning."

"A'ight, Dee," Nick said.

"Okay, baby," I said, and then we ended the call.

After Nick put his cell phone back into his pocket, he looked at me and said, "Let's get things popping."

"I'm ready," I told him.

Chapter 6

Didn't See That Coming

It took Dylan's attorney almost three hours to return Nick's call. But when Nick and I spoke with him and told him about the shooting incident between him and my father, he gave us high hopes that he was the man for the job and that he was going to handle everything. Mr. Berlinsky, Esq. was the man to know in Miami. He has represented every known, big-time drug dealer in the land. He was a very smart and well-connected Jewish attorney. He was a very expensive attorney too. Everyone in Miami knows that Mr. Berlinsky charges whatever legal fees he wants. "My retainer is ten thousand. So bring that with you when you come to court tomorrow, and I will take care of the rest," he told me.

"Okay. Thank you," I replied, and then we hung up.

"So, what do you think?" I asked Nick.

"I think he's gonna walk in that courtroom tomorrow and shut shit down," Nick said confidently.

"Well, give me the ten grand and I'll be on my way," I told him.

"I'm on it," he replied, and then he scurried off towards his bedroom.

He reappeared with the money wrapped up in a Macy's

shopping bag and handed it to me. "The lawyer's money is in there so be careful and put it away."

"Don't worry," I said and grabbed my purse from the coffee table. I stuffed the bag of money down into my purse and zipped it up.

"So are you going back to your apartment?"

"Yes," I began to say. "I need to get in my Jacuzzi tub and take a long, hot bath."

"Want me to follow you home?"

"No, I'm good."

"You know Dylan would kill me if he knew I let you leave my apartment alone this time of night."

"If you don't tell him, then I won't either." I smiled, and then I turned and walked towards the front door.

"Well, call me as soon as you get home," he instructed me.

"Okay. I can do that." I smiled once again and then I left.

I couldn't sleep a wink after I took a long, hot bath and got into bed. I tossed and turned all night. So, when I finally saw sunlight peer through the blinds of my bedroom window, I got out of bed and started my day with ease.

It was six o'clock in the morning. So, I had three hours of free time before I had to meet Dylan's attorney at court. I wrestled with the idea that Mr. Berlinsky might not be able to spring Dylan out of jail because of the fact that my father's name carried weight around the courts in Miami-Dade County. My father made it perfectly clear that if I didn't roll with him, then I could kiss Dylan goodbye.

After an hour and a half passed, my cell phone started ringing. I knew it had to be Dylan calling me to make sure his attorney and I would be at court this morning. So I answered his call on the second ring. "Hello," I said anxiously.

"Hi, Kira, this is Sonya," Dylan's sister said.

Caught off guard with her call, I hesitated before I uttered another word. "Um, uh, who is this?" I asked, even though I already knew who it was. I did this to prolong the inevitable. I knew she was calling my cell phone to speak with Dylan. She would always call my cell phone when Dylan wouldn't answer his phone.

"This is Sonya, girl."

"Oh, hey. What's up?"

"I'm trying to get in touch with Dylan. I've been trying to get him on the phone since last night, but his phone keeps going straight to voicemail. Is he there with you?"

"No. He's not here. Is there something I can help you with?" I asked her.

"Girl, Bruce has put his fucking hands on my mama again."

"Please tell me you're joking."

"No, I am not. My mother is in the fucking kitchen making herself a cup of coffee with a black eye."

"Oh my God! Where is Bruce?"

"I think he left and went to work. But I told my mother it ain't gonna matter that his ass went to work because Dylan will go up there and drag his ass out on the streets when he finds out what he did to her."

"Oh my God! Are y'all gonna call the police?" I asked her.

"I started to, but I felt like Dylan needed to know what's going on before I called them."

I was shocked and at a loss for words hearing about Bruce giving Mrs. Daisy a black eye. Dylan was going to flip out when he found out about this. Too bad he wasn't around right now to handle this mess. So, now I was going to have to break the news to Sonya that he was in jail. I cleared my throat, and then I said, "Dylan is going to kill me for telling you this, but he's in jail. But he's going in front of a judge this morning so he can get a bond."

"Jail!? Why is he in there? And when did he get locked up?" she shouted.

"He was arrested last night because he made the mistake of shooting my father in the shoulder."

"Oh my God! Mama, Dylan is in jail!" Sonya yelled on the other end of the phone. There was no doubt that her mother heard her loud and clear.

"Hey, wait! Hold up, Sonya! Dylan didn't want your mother to know that he's in jail."

"Why didn't you tell me that?"

"I was getting ready to, but you just screamed it out without giving me any type of notice."

"Dylan's in jail?" I heard Mrs. Daisy say in the background. Her voice sounded so troubled. I wanted to kick myself for opening my big mouth. Mrs. Daisy was already going through a bunch of mess with her new husband, and now that I've added Dylan's stint in jail to her list of drama, her poor heart may give out on her. I sure wouldn't be able to forgive myself if that happened.

"Please tell her that he's coming home this morning," I instructed Sonya.

"Ma, Kira says that he's coming home this morning," she told her.

"What is he in jail for?" I heard her ask Sonya.

"Tell her that he got arrested for reckless driving," I rushed to say.

"He's in there because the cops pulled him over for driving too fast," Sonya lied.

"Dylan knows better than to drive like a maniac. He could make a mistake and have a bad accident," I heard Mrs. Daisy say. "What time does he go before the judge?"

"My mama wants to know what time does Dylan have to be in court?"

"He's on the nine o'clock docket."

"Mama, Kira said Dylan's on the docket for nine o'clock."

"Okay. Well, tell her to get down there early so she can pick up my baby. I know he's going crazy down there in that filthy jail," I heard Mrs. Daisy say.

Sonya was about to repeat what her mother said, but I told her not to because I had already heard every word she said. Sonya did tell me to have Dylan call her immediately after he gets bailed out of jail. I assured her that I would. And I also made her swear that she would keep Mrs. Daisy away from Bruce until Dylan and I got over there to see her. Sonya promised me that she would do just that.

Chapter 7

Case #389740-98121

I arrived at the Miami-Dade courthouse by 8:30 a.m. I parked my car and headed into the building so I could have a meeting with Attorney Berlinsky. He was waiting in one of the attorney and client conference rooms next to courtroom B. When I walked in the door he stood up to his feet and gave me a handshake. "You must be Kira," he said.

I smiled. "And you must be Mr. Berlinsky," I replied.

"Yes, I am," he agreed and then we both took a seat.

I took a good look at Mr. Berlinsky. He was definitely representing his Jewish culture. He wore the black kippah on top of his head. His suit attire was a pair of black pants, a plain white shirt, and a black coat. He wasn't flashy at all. "So, did you bring in the retainer fee?" he didn't hesitate to ask.

"Yes, I did," I said and removed the shopping bag filled with money from my purse. After I handed him the bag, he pulled out the money to look it over.

"Don't worry. It's all there," I assured him.

He cracked a smile. "Oh, I'm not worried about that," he told me while he began to put the money back into the bag.

"So, have you had a chance to see Dylan yet?" I wanted to know.

"No, I haven't. I wanted to see you first and handle this part. And then I was going to visit him afterward."

"So, do you know who's gonna be his judge?"

"Yes, he's going in front of Judge Anderson."

"Is he tough?"

"He's been on the bench for over twenty years, so he has his good and bad days."

"How do you think he's going to react in Dylan's case, knowing that he shot a retired judge?"

"Well, see, the good thing about Dylan is, he's not a career criminal. The fact that he hasn't been in trouble before will definitely help him."

"Well, how much do you think the judge is going to set his bond at?" I continued to question this guy. Shit, I needed some answers.

"It shouldn't be more than fifty thousand. And with a bail bondsman, all you would have to fork over is most likely half of that."

"Okay. Well, let's do it," I said eagerly. I wanted to see my baby. And even though it had only been sixteen hours since I'd seen him, I missed him dearly.

—————

Inside the courtroom, Mr. Berlinsky escorted me to my seat and then he disappeared behind a wooden door not too far from the benches where police officers were assigned to sit. I assumed that was where they were housing Dylan.

Not much longer after he disappeared, he reappeared, and then he took a seat behind one of the two tables that were placed in front of the judge's chair. "All rise, the honorable Judge Anderson is presiding," the courtroom deputy announced to the jam-packed courtroom.

I looked up at the judge with his salt-and-pepper, balding

head, and his little beady eyes. He looked like a sincerely nice gentleman. So, I knew Dylan, and Mr. Berlinsky had it in the bag.

"You may take a seat," the judge said, and then he went into his spiel about whoever wanted to reschedule their court dates so they could hire counsel needed to form a line.

I watched him intently as he went through each case. He was giving out bonds and letting people go home left and right. Today had started off right.

"Next case," he said. And that's when Attorney Berlinsky stood up and approached the bench. The prosecutor followed suit while the deputy grabbed Dylan's arm and escorted him into the courtroom. Dylan quickly scanned the courtroom, and when he spotted me, he smiled. I smiled back because it was just a matter of minutes before I would be able to take him home.

"Your Honor, my client Dylan Callender is seeking a bond today so he can keep his job and properly prepare to clear his name from all the charges brought against him."

"Do you have anything to say?" the judge asked the prosecutor.

"Your Honor, I ask the court that you deny Mr. Callender a bond because he not only shot a human being, he almost took the life of a retired judge that presided over this very courtroom, over drugs. We can't let this man back onto the streets. I have no doubts that if we do let Mr. Callender go home, who's to say that he won't try to harm the victim again?" the prosecutor stated.

My heart tumbled into the pit of my stomach after I heard the prosecutor rip Dylan a new asshole. This man wasn't fucking playing. He came in here with intentions to bury Dylan and so far he was achieving that goal.

"Your Honor, my client has never been in trouble before. He has a clean record up until this point. He's not a danger to our society in the least bit. May I also add that he's engaged to the victim's daughter? She can attest to my client's character, and she's in the courtroom right now," Mr. Berlinksy commented, and then he turned around and pointed at me. I raised my hand briefly and smiled.

The judge and the prosecutor both looked at me. It felt like they could see directly through me. "Your Honor, having the victim's daughter testify to his character would be biased. Who's to say that she wasn't coerced to be here?" the prosecutor said.

"He's making mere assumptions, Your Honor. We can clearly see that this young lady is here on her own merit," Mr. Berlinsky interjected.

The judge cleared his throat and began to speak. The courtroom was pin-drop quiet. "Enough, gentlemen," the judge huffed. "With all the evidence I have in front of me, it is my decision to deny Mr. Callender bail at this time," he concluded, and then he said, "Bailiff, take the prisoner back to the holding cell."

The deputy grabbed ahold of Dylan's arm and escorted him back out of the courtroom. Dylan looked at me one last time and blew me a kiss. "Call me," I whispered, even though I knew he couldn't hear me, but I knew he could read lips.

"Next case," I heard the judge say, which was my cue to exit the courtroom.

I was literally bummed out by the judge's decision not to give my baby a bond. But in the back of my mind, I had already known things would be like this. Once he found out that Dylan shot a retired judge, that motherfucker had already made up his mind while he was in his chambers that he wasn't letting Dylan out of jail. It wouldn't surprise me if this fucking judge were a friend of my father's.

I sucked my teeth and cursed underneath my breath. I even gritted on the prosecutor when he looked back at me after the judge sealed Dylan's fate. He gave me a half smile. I knew he was being smug with me, but it was cool. He may have won the battle now, but my baby would come out on the winning end when the battle was over.

When I got up to leave, Mr. Berlinsky pulled me to the side so he and I could talk. "I just want to let you know that I spoke to Dylan before the bailiff took him out of the courtroom and he's decided that he wants to appeal the judge's decision to deny him bail. So, I'm heading over to the clerk's office now to file the motion to appeal it."

"How long does that process take?"

"Not long. Once I file the motion, it should only take a day or so to get another court date. I'm shooting for a bail hearing no later than Friday."

"So, Dylan's gonna get back in court by Friday?" I asked with excitement. I needed some clarity.

"Yes. So, call me tomorrow afternoon, and I'll have more information for you then."

"Okay. Thanks, Mr. Berlinsky," I said and shook his hand.

I can say that even though I was down about my baby not getting out of jail today, I can say that I'm feeling optimistic once again.

Chapter 8

Time to Break the News

As soon as I got into my car, I called Nick and gave him the bad news. "You are not going to believe it."

"What happened?"

"The judge denied his bail."

"Why? He's not a flight risk."

"I know. But that's not how the judge and the prosecutor saw him."

"What did they say?"

"Well, they argued that Dylan shot my father over drugs. So you know, they turned their noses up when they looked at all the evidence and found out that my dad was a retired judge."

"Isn't that discrimination?"

"I don't know what it is. But I do know that they are not playing fair, so Mr. Berlinsky is in the clerk's office filing a motion to appeal the judge's decision. So hopefully, Dylan will be out of jail by the end of the week."

"Did you get to see him?"

"Yes, I saw him. He smiled at me when he came into the courtroom. But when the deputy was taking him away, he looked so disappointed."

"How do you think the attorney did?"

"I felt like he could have said more in Dylan's defense. But overall, I think he did okay. The real test will come when he goes back into court for Dylan's second bail hearing."

"So what are you about to do now?"

"I'm going to run over to Dylan's mother's house to check on her because Sonya called me this morning and told me that Bruce hit her again."

"Man, you've got to be pulling my fucking leg right now."

"No, I am not. And it gets worse."

"Whatcha mean?"

"He gave her a fucking black eye this time."

"Oh hell no! Is that nigga crazy?!" Nick roared. "Yo, Kira, don't say another word. I'm on my way, and I will meet you there in fifteen minutes."

"Hold up, Nick, wait!" I said. But I was too late. Nick had already disconnected our call. Nick was Dylan's right-hand man. He loved Mrs. Daisy like she was his mother. So it didn't surprise me that Nick was going to pay a visit to Bruce. For Bruce's sake, I hoped he wasn't there because shit was about to hit the fan.

<hr />

While en route to Mrs. Daisy's house I tried calling Sonya, but she didn't answer her cell phone. I texted her and left her a voicemail message letting her know that I was on my way to her mother's house, and so was Nick.

It only took me a matter of twenty minutes to get there from the courthouse. As I pulled up curbside in front of Mrs. Daisy's house, I noticed that Sonya's car was gone. But Mrs. Daisy's and Bruce's cars were in the driveway. "Sonya, where the hell are you?" I mumbled while I dialed her cell phone number again. After the fifth ring, her voicemail picked up. "Sonya, I'm sitting outside your mother's house. I see Bruce's and your mother's car parked in the driveway. So, please call me back because I told Nick what happened to your mom and he's pissed. He told me he was on his way here now. And you know I'm not gonna be able to get between Nick and Bruce once shit gets heated. I need some help, girl. Call me back."

Immediately after I disconnected the call, I got out of my car and headed up to the front door. I rang the doorbell twice before the front door opened. Bruce peered around the slightly ajar door. "How are you doing?" he asked.

"I'm doing fine. But I stopped by to talk to Mrs. Daisy, so can I come in?" I asked politely.

"She's taking a nap right now," he replied. But I knew he was lying.

"Well, can I come in and use the bathroom? I promise I won't wake her. I need to use it bad," I said. I was hoping he'd buy my lie because I needed to get inside the house to see if Mrs. Daisy was all right.

"Cut the act! You know you don't have to use the damn bathroom," he hissed.

"But I do. You can stand by the bathroom door and listen if you want," I volunteered. I swear I was doing everything in my power to get this asshole to let me in the house.

"Why don't you just take your lying ass on home and use the bathroom there. Cause you aren't getting in my goddamn house! Now get on out of here!" he roared, and then he slammed the front door.

As soon as Bruce slammed the door in my face, I heard Nick's black Range Rover come to a screeching halt behind me. I turned around and saw him and another guy who I remembered seeing once before today hop out of his truck. I stepped off the porch and greeted him on the sidewalk. "Is that fucking coward in the house?" he huffed.

"Yeah, he's in there. But he isn't letting anyone in the house, and he sure isn't gonna come out here, especially if he sees that you're here and you've brought some company."

"Where is Mrs. Daisy?" Nick wanted to know.

"That moron said she's in there taking a nap, but I don't believe him."

"I don't believe that shit either," Nick said, and then he raced onto the front porch. The guy he brought with him followed him onto the porch.

"What are you gonna do?" I asked while I stood in the yard and watched Nick ring the doorbell and knock on the door.

"I'm gonna make that loser let me in so I can make sure that Mrs. Daisy is all right," Nick replied. But to no avail; Bruce refused to open the door.

As Nick and the other guy exited the porch, Bruce opened up a window from the top floor and began to shout obscenities at Nick. "Get the hell off my property before I call the cops!" he threatened.

"Call the police, Bruce, because when they get here, I will personally tell them how you beat up on Mrs. Daisy," I yelled.

"I haven't done no such thing," he yelled back.

"You're a motherfucking liar!" I snapped.

"Why don't you come down here so we can have a man-to-man talk," Nick suggested. He was acting very calm, but his pleasantry didn't help.

"I'm not coming anywhere. Now I want all three of you people to get off my property!" he shouted.

"Whatcha gon' do if we don't leave?" Nick pressed the issue.

"You stand out there long enough, you'll find out," Bruce replied sarcastically.

I grabbed Nick by his arm. "Come on, Nick. He's not coming out here, so let's get out of here before he calls the cops."

"Kira, you know I don't care about the cops. My partner's mother is in that house, probably in a lot of pain, and we can't do shit about it. Do you know how Dylan would react if he was out here? He'd kick that motherfucking front door down to make sure his mom was all right."

"Yeah, you're right. But we can't do that. We've got a lot to lose," I explained to Nick.

Nick looked back up at the window where Bruce was shouting from. This time he was nowhere to be seen. "Yo, I swear if that asshole slips up and opens that door, I'm gonna kill him with my bare hands."

"I believe you, and that's why we gotta go," I said sternly as I escorted him back to his truck.

"Where is Sonya?" he wanted to know.

"I don't know. I've tried calling her a few times, but she didn't answer. She's probably somewhere with loud noises that's preventing her from hearing her phone ring."

"Well, after you get to talk to her, call me and let me know."

"All right."

After I watched Nick drive away from Mrs. Daisy's house, I started up my engine and followed suit. And as I drove away, I looked back at the house and noticed there was movement behind the curtains. There was no doubt in my mind that Bruce was staring out of the window at me. This made my blood boil. But there was nothing I could do about it. He would, however, get what's coming to him once Dylan was out of jail. I was gonna make sure of it. Fucking loser!

Chapter 9

Visitation Time

I called Mr. Berlinsky today like he told me to. I didn't get to speak with him though. I did speak with his paralegal. "I'm sorry, but Mr. Berlinsky isn't in the office. He had to leave early because of a family emergency," she said.

"Would you be able to tell me if Dylan Callender has another court date for a bail hearing?" I asked.

"Oh yes, Mr. Berlinsky was able to get a court date for this Thursday, at ten o'clock."

"Okay. Thank you very much," I said.

"You're quite welcome," she replied.

After all the drama from the day before with Mrs. Daisy's husband, Bruce, pulling me in one direction and my father pulling me in another direction, I really needed to hear some good news. This news couldn't have come at a better time. Dylan was going to be happy when I walked into that jail and told him that he has a new court date.

———————

I hated seeing my baby Dylan behind bars, but there wasn't anything I could do to get him out. My father pulled a few strings to keep my man in jail. But it's okay. Between Dylan's attorney and me, we will come up with a solution.

While I waited patiently for the correctional officer behind the desk to call me after Dylan was brought down to the visiting room, I watched and eavesdropped on another woman's visit with her boyfriend. I heard their entire conversation, and it wasn't a pleasant one. She was a black chick that looked like she was in her early twenties. She was of average height, and she was on the thin side. She wore a red weave, and she dressed like she was a stripper. Her body was covered in tattoos, and she had close to one dozen piercings on her lips, tongue, nose, belly button, and her ears. She looked a hot fucking mess, and she was loud and boisterous. The correctional officer told her to bring her volume down twice. He even told her that if he had to tell her one more time that he was going to terminate her visit. "Look Ray-Ray, I refuse to keep coming down here so you can keep disrespecting me," she argued through the phone. There was bulletproof glass separating her from him, and the only way they could communicate was through a phone that was built into the wall.

I couldn't hear what he was saying. But I could see him just as clear as day, and he was livid. He made hand gestures, and his eyes looked like they were about to pop out of his fucking head. There was no question in my mind that if he was given a chance to put his hands around her neck, he would.

"You know what, nigga? Fuck you! I'm out of here!" she shouted through the phone, and then slammed the phone onto the hook. After she stood up to her feet, she turned her ass around towards him and smacked it. "Kiss my ass too!" she shouted once more, and then she stormed off towards the exit door.

There were only two other women in the waiting room, but they heard the commotion, and they found it to be hilarious. "Boy, was she mad at him," one of the women said jokingly.

I laughed to myself because I had to remain focused. I was there to hatch out a plan with Dylan. Not feed into the drama of the inmates and their ghetto-ass girlfriends.

So finally, after waiting for fifteen minutes, Dylan was brought down to the visiting room. He was dressed in a huge orange jumpsuit, and jail-issued brown flip-flops, but that didn't matter to me. He was still a strong man in my eyes, and that wasn't going to change. "How are you?" I asked him after I smiled and put the telephone up to my ear.

"I'm all right. But I'll be even better after I get out of this fucking place."

"I know. I know. But you're gonna be fine because I just got off the phone with Mr. Berlinsky's paralegal and she said that you're set to go back to court on Thursday."

Shocked by my news, Dylan gave me a half smile. "You bull-shitting?!"

I smiled from ear to ear. "No, I am not, you're gonna be home in two days."

"Baby, I hope so, because I'm missing you like crazy. Plus, I've got a lot of moves I need to make."

"Look, don't worry about all of that. That's what Nick is there for. Trust me; he's handling everything."

"How much dough have you and Nick given him so far?"

"Well, he wanted ten grand for the retainer fee, and then he asked me for another five grand to file the motion for a new bail hearing. So, we've given him fifteen grand," I explained.

"So, have you talked to your pops again?"

"Yes, I went back up to the hospital to see him but he started acting reckless, so I left," I started off by saying. I knew I needed to choose my words wisely before something slipped out that I didn't want Dylan to know.

"You do know that he's behind me not getting out of jail?"

"Yeah. I know."

"Okay. Well then, you also know that you've got to get him

to talk to these people down here so I can get out of this fucking place."

"Baby, trust me, I'm working on it." I tried to assure him. "So where are they housing you?" I continued.

"I'm in this big-ass cell block with a lot of young cats. It's loud as hell in there, but I'll manage."

"Do you know anyone in there?"

"I know a few guys, but I'm not in here to make friends."

"Are you eating?"

"Not really. The food they serve in this shithole tastes like dog food."

"Well, hopefully, you won't be in there too much longer. That way you can get some real food into your stomach."

"Have you seen Kendrick or any of his boys?"

"No. I've been pretty much laying low. I've hardly left the house since the police arrested you."

"Good. Keep it like that. I don't want you roaming around town by yourself. Those streets aren't safe. I swear I'll kill a motherfucker if I find out someone laid a finger on you."

"Baby, don't worry. I'm gonna be fine. Nick is taking really good care of me."

"He'd better," Dylan commented. "Have you heard anything from that cop?"

"Who, the detective?"

"Yeah."

"No. He hasn't tried to contact me," I lied. Once again, I knew this was an issue I couldn't talk about right now. I needed Dylan to concentrate on getting out of jail rather than think about whether or not Detective Grimes had been trying to contact me. I figured since Nick knew what was really going on, he'd take care of that situation until Dylan came home.

"So, you're good?" he asked me again. I knew he was trying to poke at me to see if I'd break. But I held my ground and played the role because he had enough shit on his plate already.

I took a deep breath. "Yeah, I'm pretty good," I replied with a straight face.

"Has my mother or my sister tried to call you?"

I hesitated for a second. I didn't know whether to lie or tell him the truth. Dylan immediately saw the hesitation on my face. "You told them I was locked up, didn't you?"

"Yes. I spoke to Sonya, and she practically forced me to tell her where you were," I lied, trying to keep a straight face.

"But I told you not to tell them," Dylan whined.

"I know, baby. But she called and wanted to talk to you about something important. So, I had to tell her the truth."

"She didn't tell my moms, did she?"

I sighed heavily. "Yeah, she did."

"Come on, Kira; you know how much my mother worries about me. Why did you do that?" Dylan hissed. He was getting pretty irritated with me at this point. So, I knew I needed to calm him down. I also knew that telling him that Nick tried to beat Bruce's ass would be a bad idea. I figured I'd said enough for one visit, so it would behoove me to shut my damn mouth. And that's exactly what I did.

"Will you please calm down? I told Sonya to tell your mother that you were in jail because of a speeding ticket. And all she said was that you needed to slow your butt down before you have a car accident," I explained.

Dylan searched my face for a moment or two, then he said, "I appreciate you getting Sonya to cover for me. But you're gonna have to keep everything else concerning me close to the hip. My mother is already going through a lot of shit with that loser Bruce. Speaking of which, where was he when Sonya told mama I was in jail?"

"I think Sonya said he was at work."

"That bastard better be. Because if he ever puts his hands on my mama again, I'm gonna personally kill him with my bare hands."

"Dylan, please calm down."

"What did Sonya want with me anyway?" he asked.

I felt a sharp pain in my gut after Dylan questioned me about why Sonya wanted to talk to him in the first place. As bad as I wanted to tell him the truth, I knew that right now wasn't a good time to tell him that Bruce put his hands on his mother. So, I pulled a story out of the air about how she needed some money.

"How much did she need?"

"A couple of grand. So, I gave it to her."

"Okay. That's cool," he replied after he calmed down a little.

For the rest of the visit, he and I talked about how he wanted to go down to Key West for a few days once he's out on bail. I agreed that that would be a great getaway. In reality, all I wanted was for him to come home so I could hold him in my arms.

Immediately after the correctional officer announced that the visit must come to an end, I blew a kiss at Dylan, hung up the telephone, and then I stood up from my chair. He blew a kiss right back at me.

"You looking good, girl!" I heard him shout from the other side of the glass window.

"Don't worry, I'm keeping it tight for you," I commented, smiled, and then I left.

Back in my car, all I could think about was how crazy shit was going to get. I really couldn't wrap my mind around it, but I figured that if I didn't, I might find myself on the losing end.

Chapter 10

Loyalty Over Blood
Any Day

On my way home from the jail I decided to make an outgoing call to Nick, but while I was dialing his number, a call came through and interrupted it. When I realized that the call was coming from my father, I answered it even though I knew it was a bad idea to do so. "Hello," I said.

"What happened to you that prevented you from coming to see me today?" he started off.

"Daddy, I was coming by the hospital to see you, but I got tied up with some last-minute stuff," I told him.

"What kind of stuff could you have gotten tied up with that is more important than coming to see me when I am lying in a hospital bed with a gunshot wound inflicted by your gangster boyfriend?" he roared.

"Daddy, I'm really not trying to get into an argument with you."

"I'm not arguing, Kira!" he snapped. "I'm trying to get you to understand that you're always putting other things before me. Now how would you feel if I'd done the same to you?"

"I'd be upset," I replied nonchalantly.

"Exactly. So, why don't you treat me with a little more respect and find some time in your busy schedule to come to the hospital to see me."

"I'll come up there if you promise not to bring up Dylan's name during the visit."

"Isn't he the reason I am here?"

"Daddy, you're starting to argue with me again."

"Kira, I am not arguing with you. I'm only giving you the facts."

"Well, I don't wanna talk about that situation. I'm staying neutral, and that's it."

"So, you're telling me that you're siding with that monster?" my father barked.

"Look, Dad; I can't do this with you anymore." I cut him off. "I'm on my way up to the hospital to see you. But I'm warning you now that if you try to force me to talk about Dylan, I'm gonna leave. Understood?"

"Yeah, whatever," he replied, and then he slammed the phone down on the base. The line went completely dead.

Under normal circumstances, I would've been upset. But since I knew why he was acting this way, I gave him a pass.

Chapter 11

Having Second Thoughts

I had major reservations about going to the hospital to see my dad. The stress that he had put on me had become unbearable. But like the trooper I am, I decided to go against my better judgment, and now I was heading west to pay him a visit.

I was happy to see that the hospital was pretty quiet. There was only a doctor and a few nurses on staff, but they seemed fairly busy at their station. I waved at them and continued on to my dad's room.

He was watching television when I walked in. "What are you watching?" I asked.

"Actually, the TV is watching me," he said jokingly and cracked a smile.

I took a seat in a chair next to his bed. "So how are you feeling?"

"Everything is good until my painkillers wear off."

"What are they giving you?"

"Vicodin."

"Oh, wow! I'm surprised you're not sleeping."

"I was asleep a while ago. As soon as I woke up, I called you."

"What did you eat for dinner?"

"I ate a bowl of chicken soup and a couple of crackers."

"Have they said when you would be discharged?"

"Yeah, I spoke to the doctor earlier, and he said that I should be clear to go home tomorrow. So, I was wondering if you wouldn't mind picking me up and taking me home?"

"Sure. I can do that," I told him.

"So, how are things with you?"

"I'm fine. I just had a lot of errands to run today, so I'm a little tired. But after I get some rest tonight, I'll be fine in the morning."

"You know the cops found that girl's body," he whispered as he changed the subject. It came out of thin air.

"What girl?" I asked, trying to play naïve. But I knew who he was talking about.

"The one we saw get killed."

"Daddy, are you fucking kidding me right now?" I barked. This guy was literally trying to back me into a corner so I would admit that I saw Nancy get killed.

"Come on now; you can't talk to me like that. I am your father," he barked back. "All I was trying to do was tell you the good news."

"You thought that was good news?"

"Well, if it wasn't good news to you, then I'm sure it was good news to her parents, because now they have closure."

I stood up from the chair. "Daddy, I can't do this with you anymore."

"What do you mean, you can't do this with me? You said you didn't want to talk about Dylan. So, I'm honoring your wishes. But then when I bring up the conversation about the young lady that you and I witnessed getting killed, you get upset about that too. I can't win for losing."

At that moment, I knew something was wrong with my father. He was trying too hard to get me to confess that I was with him when he saw Nancy being killed. So, I reached over and snatched the bedsheets back from my father, and lo and behold, he had a recording device, along with a microphone tied to his waist. I swear, I almost gasped for air.

The look on his face showed me a different side of him. "What is this, Daddy?" I asked him, even though I already knew what it was. I just needed him to utter the words himself.

"What, this?" he asked as he pointed to the recording device.

"Yes, that," I said as I stood over him.

"Look, Detective Grimes told me to wear this," he began to explain, but I cut him off midsentence.

"Enough, Daddy, I don't wanna hear another word! I'm out of here!" I shouted and then I stormed out of his room.

When I entered back into the hallway, Detective Grimes appeared from the room next to my father's room. I looked at him and rolled my eyes. "You're fucking pathetic to use an old man to do your dirty work!" I commented, and then I made my way to the elevator.

Immediately after I got off the elevator, I rushed to my car and got the hell out of there. I started to go home, but my nerves were too bad for me to be alone, so I decided to go over to Nick's place, but I needed to make sure he was home first before I made that long drive.

"Are you home?" I asked after I pulled out of the parking garage and called him.

"No, I'm out South Park. Why?"

"Because we need to talk."

"Are you okay?"

"Not really. But I will be okay as soon as I figure out what I need to do."

"Well, I'm in the middle of something, so can you come out this way?"

"Sure. What's the address?"

"I'm at 2084 Atlantic Drive. So, after you park your car, ring the buzzer and I'll buzz you in."

"Okay. Well, I'm on my way."

"Cool."

Chapter 12

The Hideout Location

After Nick gave me the address to where he was, I programmed it in my GPS device and drove straight there. With everything going on in my mind it just dawned on me that I was going to Nick's little private getaway. No one knew of this apartment but Dylan and me. So after I was let into his sanctuary, it didn't surprise me to see them counting a butt load of cash at his kitchen table.

"I can take some of that off your hands if you want me to," I said, in hopes that it would take my mind off the sneaky shit my father just pulled on me.

"Sure, why not?" He smiled. "So, what's up?" he didn't hesitate to say while he stacked one-hundred-dollar bills on a money-counting machine.

I took a seat at the kitchen table across from him. "I've got to figure out what to do with my father."

"What's going on?"

"Well, you know, I've been out running all day trying to get things situated with the attorney so Dylan can get another bail hearing. Okay, so while I was leaving the jail after seeing Dylan, my father calls me and starts fussing about why I hadn't been to the hospital to see him. So I went into this spiel about how

WIFEY'S NEXT DEADLY HUSTLE / 49

busy I'd been all day and that as soon as I found the time I was going to come to see him. Well, he didn't like my answer and started talking about how he wouldn't be in the hospital if it weren't for my gangster drug dealer shooting him."

"What?!"

"That's not it. He even went below the belt and said that he doesn't like the fact that I'm putting Dylan before him. So, he and I started going back and forth until I stopped him in his tracks and told him that I wasn't going to keep arguing with him. I also told him that I would come by and see him, but he had to promise me that we weren't going to discuss Dylan. So, he agreed to do that. But when I get there, he starts talking about that chick I used to work with named Nancy."

"Are you fucking kidding?!"

"No. And after he brought her name up, he said, "You know the cops found her body, right?"

"Nooooooo."

"Yes, he did. And then he tried to get me to admit that I was with him when Kendrick's boys shot her in the fucking head! I swear I was so fucking pissed that I stood up and asked him what his freaking problem was? And before I gave him a chance to answer me, I pulled back his bedsheets and saw that he was wearing a fucking recording device and a wire. So, I started screaming at him. And then he starts accusing Detective Grimes, saying that he made him wear the wire. So, I leave the room and guess who I see coming out of the room next to my father's room?"

"That fucking cop?"

"Yep. So, I grit on him, and then I called him pathetic."

"What did he say?"

"I didn't give that bastard time to do anything. I just walked off and got the hell out of there."

"Yo, Kira, I'm sorry to say this, but your pops gotta go. We can't have that. If he brings you and Dylan down, then I'm gonna be affected too. So, we've gotta do something about him now."

"What are we going to do? What do you mean, get rid of him?" I wondered aloud.

"We've gotta put him out of his misery, or else he's gonna put all of us in jail. I've got too much shit to live for out here than to be in jail. That's not how I want to spend the rest of my days."

"So, in other words, you're telling me that we've gotta kill him?"

"Yeah, because let's face it, your father has a lot of clout in the court system, so it doesn't matter how much money we give Mr. Berlinsky, no one is going to give Dylan a bond. And Mr. Berlinsky knows this as well. But he's not gonna tell us that because it's about the money. The more money we put in his hands, the more he's obligated to make you feel optimistic about beating this case."

"So, you're essentially saying that it's a waste of time to give Berlinsky any more money?"

"No, Kira, I'm saying that the only way Dylan is going to get out of jail and the cops getting off your ass is if we close your father's mouth once and for all. But if you don't mind the cops harassing you, and visiting Dylan in jail, then act like you haven't heard a word I've said. But please bear in mind that I have a lot at risk, so I'm gonna have to cut ties with you because I can't afford to have that type of heat on me," Nick said coldheartedly.

I thought for a minute about what Nick said, and it made perfect sense. But how was I going to get up the nerve to agree to have my father killed? That's kind of fucked up if you look at it from a *blood is thicker than water* scenario. But then when I realized all the shit I have gotten mixed up in since Judge Mahoney was first killed, I figured that cutting my ties with him wouldn't be so bad. That way I wouldn't have to worry about looking over my shoulders for Kendrick and his boys or the cops. It would be a win-win for Dylan, Nick, and myself.

"If I agree with you and say yes, then who's gonna kill him?" I asked.

"I'm sorry, Kira, but I can't tell you that. That's going against the rules Dylan and I live by."

"Okay. Well, will you make sure that whoever does it, does it quickly? I don't want him to die a slow and painful death."

"Okay. I can do that."

"Good."

Chapter 13

These Assholes Aren't Worth Shit

It had been two days since I saw or talked to my father. That stunt he pulled on me was an act that I couldn't forgive him for. I didn't tell him that. In fact, the day after he was released from the hospital he called and left me a voicemail message telling me that he was home and that he was going to need a nurse to care for him. But before he called one, he needed to ask me would I come by his home and help him with his recovery efforts. I didn't call him back because I just didn't want to deal with him at that moment. I had to concentrate on Dylan's bail hearing. After I dealt with that, then I'd call him.

Here I was finally back in court with Dylan, crossing my fingers that he'd get a bond. We were in front of a different judge, so I felt good about that. Unlike Nick, I was pretty optimistic about my baby coming home. So, as the deputy escorted him back into court, Mr. Berlinsky and the prosecutor started going toe-to-toe about why Dylan should and shouldn't be released on bail.

Mr. Berlinsky assured the judge that Dylan wouldn't be a danger to society and that it was necessary for him to be free so he could better prepare for his trial. But then the prosecutor stated that Dylan would be a danger to society and to my father. "Your Honor, I think he needs to stay in jail during his trial," he said.

Anxiety engulfed me at that very moment. And all I could think about was how my world would turn upside down if Dylan wasn't released from jail. I can't be out there all by myself. I needed him home so he could protect me.

Once again the judge looked down at the evidence in front of him. A few seconds later, he looked back up, giving Dylan all of his attention. "Do you work, Mr. Callender?" the judge asked him.

"Yes, sir."

"And where do you work?"

"I'm self-employed. I work out of my house."

"Doing what?"

"I'm a nightclub promoter. I hire celebrities to make appearances at nightclubs. And after I pay them, I collect all of the money from the door," he said, and even though what he was saying was a lie, I was convinced otherwise.

"So, you're saying that you can do this business anywhere?"

"Yes sir, Your Honor."

"Okay. Well, I'm going to deny bail at this time since there's no danger in you losing your job."

"But Your Honor, he may not lose his job, but he has other obligations that would require him to be on the streets," Mr. Berlinsky interjected.

"I'm sorry, but my decision has been made," the judge said while he was scribbling something on the document in front of him. A couple of seconds later he handed the document to the court clerk seated next to him.

The prosecutor walked away from the bench while Mr. Berlinsky said a few words to Dylan. After he was done talking to him the deputy escorted Dylan back out of the courtroom. I waved and blew a kiss at him before he disappeared behind the wooden door.

Devastated by the judge's decision, I stood to my feet and exited the courtroom. While I was walking down the hallway, all I could think about was how right Nick was about the politics of this court system. They aren't letting Dylan get out on bail, and Mr. Berlinsky knows it.

While I was cursing him out in my mind, he rushed up behind me and tapped me on my shoulder. "Hey Kira, where are you rushing off to?" he asked me while he was panting.

"I've got somewhere to be, and I don't want to be late," I lied.

"Well, why don't you call me later so we can get the ball rolling on Dylan's trial. Think you can stop by my office sometime next week?" he asked me.

"Yeah, I'll call you and let you know."

"And do you think that you can talk to your father and maybe get him to change his story about finding the drugs and say that Dylan shot him by accident?"

"At this point, Mr. Berlinsky, I can't call it."

"Well, it would help Dylan's case out tremendously."

"All I can do is try," I said because I knew what he was asking me to do was impossible. My father wasn't going to change his story. He told me he was going to make an example out of Dylan and I believed him.

"Sounds great. See you then," he said, and then he walked off.

Boy, was I freaking pissed off. Here I just gave that cracker fifteen thousand dollars, and Dylan didn't get shit from it. Talk about getting fucked in the ass!

During my drive away from the courthouse, I called Nick. "Hey, how did court turn out?" he asked me.

"You were right. They denied Dylan's bail again."

"So, what is the plan now? What is the attorney saying?"

"He wants me to come by his office so we can talk. He also wants me to talk to my father because he feels that it may help Dylan out in the long run. But that's another issue. Are you at home?"

"Yeah, I just got here."

"Can I come over?"

"Sure. Come on."

Chapter 14

It All Comes Down To This

Nick's vibe was a little off when I entered his apartment. He went straight into killer mode when we started talking about Dylan's case. "Have you spoken to your pops since he got out of the hospital?"

"No. But he called and left me a message."

"Do you know where he is? Have the cops put him in witness protection yet?"

"I don't think so, because when he left me a message he said that he was home and that he needed a nurse to come by and help him with his recovery process."

"Well, this is what I want you to do," he said, and then he fell silent. "I'm gonna drive you over there tonight. And when we get there, I want you to go inside his house and bring him back out to the car so we can take him to a secluded spot where no one will see us."

"Is that when he's gonna get killed?"

"Do you wanna know the truth?"

"Yes, of course."

"Will you be able to handle it?"

"Yes."

"Well, yeah, that's exactly what's gonna happen. Remember, we've got to do this thing fast before he turns on all of us."

I became numb after Nick laid out his plans to take my father's life. So, I asked myself was I really ready to face the inevitable?"

"All right, let's do it," I finally said.

Nick smiled and said, "That's my girl!"

After I gave Nick the green light, he got on the phone and made a call. He excused himself from the room and went off into his bedroom.

I looked at the clock and noticed that it was almost four o'clock in the afternoon. And in a few more hours it would be nightfall. And by this time tomorrow, my father wouldn't be alive anymore. So I had to ask myself, what kind of monster had I become?

Chapter 15

It's Either Life or Death

My father was shocked when I popped up at this home. Thank God he was there alone. He had on his pajamas and his house slippers when he opened the front door. "Why did you change the locks on the front door?" I asked him after I realized I couldn't use my old keys.

"It's a long story, sweetheart!" he said, and then he changed the subject. "I'm so happy to see you." He grabbed ahold of my hand.

"Daddy, I'm gonna do whatever it is that you want me to do concerning Nancy and Dylan. But, we're gonna have to have a talk about what I'm gonna get out of all of this."

"Okay. So, when do you want to have this talk?"

"Now. So, come with me outside. That way I don't have to worry about your house being wired and our conversation being recorded."

"Well, I guess I can do that," he said, and then he turned in the opposite direction and started walking.

"Where are you going?"

"To get my coat."

"Daddy, you don't need your coat. Trust me, we won't be

gone long, plus we're gonna be sitting inside that truck while we're talking."

"Okay. Well, I guess that'll be okay," he said, and then he held his hand out for me to help him walk out of the house.

I took his hand and escorted him out to the truck. And after I helped him get into the back seat, I ran around the truck and hopped in on the opposite side. "Who are you?" I heard him ask Nick.

"I'm just her driver," Nick lied.

"You look like that man that brought those drugs to her boyfriend."

"No, sir. That wasn't me," Nick replied as he looked at my father through the rearview mirror.

"Are you sure? Because I swear you look just like that man."

"Daddy, that's not Dylan's friend."

"Well, he sure looks like him."

"Daddy, just sit back and enjoy the ride."

"I didn't know that we were leaving. Stop the car, so I can lock my front door."

"It's okay, Daddy; we're only going down the block. No one is gonna know that your front door is unlocked."

"Now you know I don't like leaving my house unattended to."

"Everything's gonna be fine," I assured him. "Drive off," I instructed Nick.

Nick sped off the gravel in my father's driveway, kicking up dirt particles and jerking my father around in the back seat. "Will you tell him to stop driving like a freaking maniac?" my father huffed.

"Calm down. He only did it so the tires won't get stuck," I lied as Nick drove away.

"Where are we going?"

"Somewhere quiet so we can talk."

"Let's talk now. I'm tired of dancing around the truth. You

and I both know that your boyfriend is a drug dealer and that he shot me to keep my mouth closed. And let's not forget when you told me that you gave those thugs Judge Mahoney's home address so they could kill him!" my father roared.

"Don't put words in my mouth. You know that's not how it happened," I snapped. I had had enough of my father's mouth. It was time for me to shut him up once and for all. "Pull over to this lake," I instructed Nick while my father was still talking.

I swear, I never thought that I'd be faced with this type of challenge. My father was all I had. But then he decided to turn his back on me so what is a girl to do? He promised to testify against Dylan and me. That meant that I was going to join Dylan behind bars. I wasn't built for that type of shit. So, I refused to be taken down. I'd rather die first.

Nick stayed in the driver's seat of the black Suburban while my father and I sat in the back. He kept a close watch on me through the rearview window while my father and I talked. "I am glad you decided to come to your senses," he started off. "Detective Grimes said that he's going to take care of both of us. He also said that as soon as the trial is over, they're going to change our identities and relocate us somewhere northwest. I'm assuming it'll be Colorado or Seattle, Washington. I'm not fond of their cold weather, but it would just have to do."

His face was bright, and it had a glow. There was no doubt in his mind that things were going to work out, especially since I assured him that I would go along. What he didn't know was that I had no intentions to go anywhere. I was tired of running from place to place. And I was tired of dealing with cops. So, how in the hell was I going to live under protective custody, knowing all of this?

"Daddy, I'm not going into witness protection with you," I finally admitted.

Shocked by my words, he said, "What do you mean you're not going into witness protection with me? You promised."

"I'm sorry, Daddy. But I'm not gonna testify against Dylan."

"Kira, are you fucking mad?" he snapped. "You gave me your word."

"I know I did, Daddy. But I lied. I have no intentions whatsoever of testifying against Dylan. I love him."

"So, you're gonna turn your back on your old man for a street thug?" he roared. The veins in the temple area of his face looked like they were going to burst.

"Yes, I am, Daddy," I said calmly, and then I grabbed the gun Nick gave me earlier from my handbag and pointed it directly at my father's head.

Taken aback by my actions, my father became irate. "So what, you're gonna shoot me now? You're gonna kill your father?" he screamed.

"I'm sorry, Daddy," I said, and then I pulled the trigger. *BOOM!*

With one bullet, my father's blood, and brain and skull tissue, splattered all over the car seats and back windows of the truck. I immediately got out of the back seat and Nick followed suit. "Torch it," I instructed him.

"I'm on it," he replied and grabbed the can of gasoline in the trunk of the truck.

I watched him as he emptied the gas can all over the truck, and then he threw a match on it. I stood a ways back and watched the truck and my father's remains go up in smoke. I knew it was sadistic of me to do what I did to my father. But he gave me no choice.

It was either life or death in my eyes!

Chapter 16

What Happens Next?

Nick and I stood there as the truck went up in flames with my father's lifeless body inside. Before we walked away from the blaze, Nick advised me to wipe my father's blood from my face with the jacket I was wearing and throw it into the fire. After I did just that, he and I turned around and walked away, and we never looked back once. We knew we had to hurry and get away from the crime scene before the officers and the fire and rescue got there. It was the only smart thing to do.

"Are you all right?" Nick asked me about a half mile into our walk away from the burn site.

"No, but I will be," I told him as we walked the long road back to the parking lot of the IHOP restaurant where we left his Range Rover. "We should've parked your truck closer. This walk is becoming too much," I retorted.

"It's not that bad. We're almost there," Nick said as we both navigated down the back road of a light marsh area. Thankfully, the water levels on some parts along this road weren't deep. Allowing alligators to eat me up for dinner was not on my list of things to do tonight.

"I hope God doesn't send me to hell for what I just did," I commented.

"Just look at it as a sacrifice. Your father was creating a hostile environment and now that he's no longer around to testify against Dylan, the judge on his case has to let him go."

"You do know that that detective is going to be all over my ass once he finds out my father is dead?"

"I'm already two steps ahead of you. You're gonna have to lawyer up ASAP. That way you can prevent the officers from harassing you."

"Think I should leave town?"

"That's the last thing you should do. That'll give them all the more reason to think that you had something to do with it. What you want to do is act like you're grieving. Act like you're gonna be lost without your father and they will have no choice but to believe that Kendrick ordered this hit."

"What if what you're saying doesn't work?"

"Look, just call a lawyer tomorrow and they'll make sure the officers don't come within a hundred feet of you."

"I wonder what Dylan is going to say after he finds out that my father is dead and that I was the one that killed him?"

"Well, if it were me, I'd be happy as fuck. I know it took a lot for you to do that since that was your pops, but at the end of the day you and Dylan will be much happier."

"I hope Dylan appreciates what I did for him."

"Oh, don't worry, he will," Nick said, and then immediately our attention was diverted to a flashing light coming in our direction.

"Oh shit! Somebody called 911." I panicked. Nick grabbed me by the arm and pulled me behind a group of trees that was big enough to hide us both.

As soon as I laid eyes on the fire and rescue vehicle and the officers that followed, I instantly felt sick on my stomach. And while standing there, the reality and gravity of his murder settled into my mind. My father was dead. Poof! Just like that, he was gone. And it was at the hands of me. No one else's. Now how was I gonna ever live in peace, knowing this?

"We're gonna have to get out of here fast," Nick told me after the last cop car passed us.

In a flash, Nick grabbed me by the arm again and pulled me in another direction to avoid being seen by anyone. We started walking towards a wooded area. "Wait, I don't think we should go that way," I told him, pointing in a different direction.

"Well, would you rather walk that way and risk being seen by the officers?" Nick asked me as he pointed towards the road.

I let out a long sigh. "If a snake bites me, I'm gonna kill you," I told him.

"Don't worry! I gotcha!" he assured me.

———⯈⬝⬝⯇———

It took Nick and me a total of seventeen minutes to get back to his truck. Immediately after we crawled inside of it, a police vehicle drove slowly by Nick's SUV. We noticed that there were two police officers inside the vehicle. At one point we thought that they were going to stop but then they continued to drive away. "Did you see that?" I asked him, paranoid as hell.

"Yeah, I did," he replied as he carefully started the ignition and put it in reverse. He backed his SUV out of the parking space and then put it in drive. "Do you see them?" Nick asked me.

"No, I don't. But I think they drove around to the back of the restaurant," I told him, unsure about the information I was giving him.

"Well, keep your eyes open," he instructed me. But it was too late; the officers had circled back around the IHOP restaurant at a moment's notice and were able to get behind Nick's truck while he was driving away. "Fuck! They're behind us,"

Nick spat. He became very nervous and it only took a millisecond for it to happen.

Nick was a very strong-minded guy. He never allowed anyone to intimidate him, and that included Dylan. See, Nick was as gangster as gangster could get. So, to see him out of that element made me see another side of him. In a situation like this, you were always supposed to be cool. Never overreact. And never let the officers see you sweat, either. But if for some reason, you let them see you with your pants down, just know that you're putting yourself in a risky situation.

"Whatcha gon' do?" I wondered aloud, as I continued to look forward. I couldn't let the officers see sudden movement or catch me looking back at them, so I remained calm until Nick figured out what we were going to do next.

"For right now, I'm gonna keep driving until they try to pull me over," he managed to say calmly.

"Do you think they suspect that we are the cause of torching the truck with my father in it?" I asked him. I became extremely nervous about the fact that there was a possibility that we could be pulled over and arrested. I could feel my entire body vibrating with tremors. My chest was heaving up and down and I could barely move my feet once Nick told me that the officers were following us. I instantly started regretting ever killing my father and leaving his burning body in that stolen SUV. How could I have been so stupid?

"If they did they would've pulled us over by now," Nick replied.

"Well, what do you think they're doing?"

"They're probably running the license plates on my truck."

"Are the tags on your truck legit?" I asked him.

Before Nick answered me, the officers turned on their blue and white lights and flipped on their sirens. "Oh my God! They know one of us killed my father!" I panicked.

"Kira, calm down! They don't know anything." Nick tried

to give me a pep talk. But it didn't work. I became unraveled at the seams. I was a ball of nerves. My stomach was doing somersaults, literally. My body was so tense it felt like I was coming down with the flu. But at the same time, I was craving a cigarette and I didn't even smoke regularly. Anything that would've calmed my raggedy nerves, I would've taken it at that moment.

Nick pulled his truck over and waited for the officers to approach us. "If they try to separate us and ask us what we were doing out here, tell 'em we came to IHOP to get something to eat but got into an argument and decided at the last minute that we weren't going inside," Nick coached me.

"What if they ask me what were we arguing about?" I questioned him.

"Tell 'em the argument was about me cheating," Nick instructed me. He ran over the spiel in the nick of time. Both officers were within a few feet of the driver and passenger side of the truck.

They drew their flashlights on us with one hand while they placed their other hand near their firearm. They were both Caucasian male police officers with chips on their shoulders. "Let me see your license and registration," the officer on the driver's side demanded.

"Sure," Nick told him and reached into the glove compartment to retrieve the registration. After he grabbed the registration, he handed it to the officer, along with his driver's license.

The officer standing on my side of the truck remained silent. He kept his eyes on me the entire time. I looked at him once and smiled. He refused to smile back.

"Officer, can you tell me why you pulled me over?" Nick wanted to know.

The officer ignored Nick's question. "Just sit tight and I will be right back," he said and then he walked away from the truck. The officer on my side didn't move a step.

My heart raced so fast my head began to hurt with a migraine. I could feel my hands trembling fiercely while the officer stood there watching Nick and me. I kept my eyes on the road in front of me. I looked at Nick through my peripheral vision a few times but neither one of us dared to talk to one another. The officer noticed that too and mentioned it. "Why are you two so quiet?" he asked us.

"I'm just—" I began to say, but Nick cut me off in midsentence. "We just had an argument, that's why we aren't talking."

"What were you two arguing about?" The officer pressed the issue.

"I found out he's cheating on me," I lied after I turned my head to face the officer.

He gave me a weird look. "I'm sorry to hear that because you're a very pretty lady."

"Me too," I replied, and then I turned my attention back towards the road in front of me.

The police officer peered around me so he could get a clear look at Nick. "I can't believe that you cheated on this beautiful lady," he said.

Nick turned his attention towards the officer and gave him the most sincere expression he could muster up. "I didn't cheat on her, sir. Trust me, it's all just a big misunderstanding."

"How long have you two been out here?" the officer wanted to know. The question came out of nowhere. I wanted to piss on myself.

"Not long," Nick answered him.

"How long is not long?" the officer inquired. But then he turned his focus back to me. "How long have you two been out here?"

I looked at Nick, hoping he'd jump in and answer the question himself. Shit, I didn't know what to say. Was this a trick question? "I don't know. Maybe twenty minutes. Maybe less,"

I finally said while I crossed my fingers and prayed that I said the right thing.

"Why you ask?" Nick questioned the officer, hoping he'd tell us what he knew.

The officer wasn't that stupid. He either knew what Nick was trying to do, or he wanted to stay a couple of steps ahead of him. "Why don't you let me ask all the questions," the officer replied sarcastically.

Before the officer could say another word, the other officer reemerged from the squad car and asked his partner to meet him in the back of Nick's SUV. I swear I was about to shit on myself. My nerves were passed frazzled; I was on the brink of a nervous breakdown. "What do you think he's saying?" I whispered to Nick.

"I don't know, so I'm gonna need you to stay calm," Nick instructed me.

I took a deep breath and exhaled. A few seconds later, the officers approached both sides of Nick's truck. The officer on Nick's side spoke first. "Sir, I'm gonna need you to step out of the vehicle."

"For what? Am I being arrested?" Nick questioned the officer.

"Sir, I'm only gonna ask you one more time to step out of the vehicle," the same officer warned.

"Listen, Officer, I'm getting out of the truck," Nick said as he pulled on the door handle to open the driver-side door, "but I still need to know if you're arresting me."

"Sir, put your hands up so we can see them!" the officer standing on my side of the truck yelled. He raised his gun and aimed it at Nick.

"Nick, please do what they say." I panicked as I watched the second officer walk around the front of the truck to assist his partner.

Nick slowly raised his hands and placed them on the steering wheel. The first officer opened the driver's-side door with this left hand and used his right hand to hold his gun while aiming it at Nick. "Step out the vehicle slowly," the officer instructed him. The second officer stood just a few feet away from his partner while he too kept his gun aimed in Nick's direction. I watched everyone closely.

"I'm getting out right now," Nick announced while he eased his way out of the driver's seat.

"Keep your hands where we can see them!" the first officer yelled.

"I am. Can't you see I got 'em up?" Nick pointed out.

"Nick, please take your time," I spoke up. I couldn't afford to let these officers put a slug in Nick's back.

Nick listened to me and stepped out of the truck with no hiccups. The officer that opened the door placed handcuffs on him and escorted him to his car. While the other officer carefully put Nick in the back seat of his squad car, the second officer walked back to my side of the car and instructed me to step out of the truck too. "Are there any weapons in this truck?" he asked me while he kept his gun aimed at me.

"No, sir," I answered quickly.

"Step out of the SUV now. And keep your hands up so I can see them," he demanded.

As instructed by the second police officer, I stepped out of Nick's truck with my hands held high. I refused to give this officer a reason to put a bullet in my head. I've seen a lot of incidents where cops have shot people for no reason. So, I wasn't gonna allow that to happen to me.

Immediately after I stepped outside Nick's truck the officer instructed me to sit on the curb near the front bumper of his squad car, so I walked over there cautiously and took a seat down on the ground. I looked inside the police vehicle to see if

I could see Nick, but I couldn't. Besides being blinded by the headlights of the police squad car, I was sitting too low on the ground.

"Make sure you keep your hands where I can see them," the same officer reminded me as he stood over me.

I wanted to make a sarcastic remark, but I refused to give him the satisfaction that he was ruffling my feathers. In my opinion, most cops were assholes with chips on their shoulders. They've always acted like they had something to prove. Tonight was no different.

Chapter 17

Close Call

I was a nervous fucking wreck sitting on the curb watching everything unfold before my eyes. While the officer was standing a few feet away from me, I'd occasionally look at him and then turn my focus to the other officer that was talking to Nick. I couldn't hear what they were saying, but I knew it was serious.

My heart continued to beat uncontrollably. All I could think about was that Nick and I were going to be arrested for my father's murder at any given second. All while Dylan was still behind bars. So, who would come and bail us out? Dylan's mother or sister? Fat chance, especially if Bruce had anything to say about it.

"You look a little nervous sitting there," the officer stated.

I tried to remain calm and hold on to my composure. I knew this dumb-ass officer was trying to play head games with me, but I wasn't about to let him see me sweat. "I'm not nervous at all," I told him, without even looking in his direction.

"So, why are your hands shaking?" he wanted to know.

I looked down at my hands and to my surprise, they were shaking. I stopped them instantly and said, "Force of habit, I do it from time to time when it's chilly outside." Then I turned my attention back towards Nick and the other officer.

"Is that the real reason?" The officer pressed the issue.

I ignored him of course.

A few minutes later, the officer talking to Nick left him sitting in the back of the police car and walked back towards the SUV. "He just gave me permission to search his vehicle," he informed the officer standing next to me.

"Don't you move an inch," the officer standing next to me warned.

I didn't respond nor did I look in his direction. I kept my sights on Nick. It was hard for me to see his face while he was sitting in the back of the police car, but that didn't stop me from looking. I needed direction from him and I needed it now.

"You search the back seat and I'll search the front," the other officer instructed his partner.

"I'm on it."

I knew both officers weren't going to find anything in Nick's truck like a gun or drugs. They were wasting their time. My biggest fear was for them to connect Nick and me to my father's murder. If for some reason they decided to take us downtown and test us for gun powder residue, then I was fucked.

While both officers searched every inch of Nick's SUV, a female officer radioed them. "Unit 527, are you guys still in the area?"

"Yes, this is Unit 527," the officer searching the front of Nick's truck answered.

"We need a 10-38. Got a ton of homeowners asking a lot of questions over here at the burn site."

Both of the officers searching Nick's truck looked at each other. "Whatcha think?" Officer one asked.

"It looks like they're clean, so I guess we can let them go," Officer two replied.

"Unit 450, this is Unit 527, we're 10-51," Officer one said.

"Unit 527, copy that," I heard the female officer say.

"Today is your lucky day," said the officer standing near me.

"It sure is," the other officer agreed and then he headed towards his squad car. He opened the back door and let Nick out. Seeing Nick's face made me feel such a relief. But I knew we weren't out of the woods yet. We still needed to get back in the truck and drive away before we let our guard down. And even then, that wasn't enough. Cops are sneaky as hell. I wouldn't put it past them if they hid wiretaps in Nick's truck, while they conducted their bogus-ass search. I mean, why did they stop us anyway? The excuse they gave us was lame as hell. But who are we? Nobody to them. They were bogus-ass police officers, and bogus-ass police officers had the authority to do anything they wanted. End of story.

After I stood up from the curb, I didn't waste any time getting back in Nick's truck. Nick got back inside his truck immediately after the officer handed him his driver's license. "Are you all right?" Nick asked me after he started up the ignition.

"Yes, I'm fine. But could we wait until we get to your place before we talk?" I suggested.

"Yeah, sure," he said and then he drove away from the police car.

———————

Nick did the speed limit the entire drive back to his apartment across town. I was a basket case and he knew it. He didn't mention it until we walked inside his apartment and locked the door behind us. I took a seat on the sofa in the living room. "Want something to drink?" he asked me after he laid his car keys on the bar area near the kitchen.

"Whatcha got?" I wanted to know.

"Effen, Svedka, Bacardi, and I got some Patrón if you want a shot of that."

"Yeah, give me a shot of Patrón. As a matter of fact, bring me the whole damn bottle. The way I feel right now, I could probably drink the whole thing," I commented.

Nick grabbed the bottle of Patrón, along with a shot glass, and brought them over to me. He set them down on the coffee table in front of me. I filled up my shot glass. Two seconds later, I had the shot glass up to my mouth, pouring every ounce of the beverage down my throat. The liquor burned my throat but it didn't stop me from pouring myself another shot. Nick got himself a beer from the refrigerator and then he took a seat on the sofa next to me. He took a couple of swallows of the beer while I downed my third shot of Patrón. "You might wanna slow down on those shots," he suggested.

"My brain is frazzled right now and this is the only thing that's calming me down," I told him.

"But you're on your fourth shot," he replied after I poured more Patrón in my shot glass.

"I'm gonna drink the entire bottle before tonight's over," I assured him.

"I can't let you do that," he said and snatched up the bottle of Patrón from the coffee table and stuffed it down in the sofa cushions next to him.

It didn't bother me that Nick took the bottle of Patrón from me. The effects of the liquor were already giving me that warm and tingling feeling. My head started feeling light and it seemed like things around me were moving in slow motion. I knew then that I was high. Without further hesitation, I poured the last bit of Patrón into my mouth, swallowed hard, and then I set the glass back down on the coffee table. I hit my chest a couple of times with a closed fist, hoping this would curtail the burning sensation in my throat, but it didn't.

"You all right?" he asked me.

"I am now," I began to say. "There was no way you could've

convinced me that we weren't going to jail tonight after those officers made us get out of your truck."

"Yeah, I thought they had us too," Nick replied.

"What was the officer saying to you while you were sitting in the back seat of his car?"

"He wanted to know how long were we in that parking lot before they saw us. Then he asked me why I smelled like gasoline."

A ball of nerves dropped into the pit of my stomach. "And what did you tell 'em?"

"I told 'em it may have happened when I was filling up my gas tank a couple of hours ago. But I knew he didn't believe me, which was why he asked me could he search my truck."

"Do you think he suspected that we had something to do with that fire? Because the other officer wanted to know if we had guns or drugs in the truck."

"He only said that to throw you off. They wanted to find out if we had anything to do with killing your pops and setting that truck on fire."

I sat there and thought for a second and that's when it hit me that Nick was right. So from this point and moving forward, we were gonna have to be on cue if the officers approached us again.

Nick continued talking about the conversation he and that officer had while he was sitting in the back of the squad car. I heard him talking, but I couldn't tell you what he was saying if you asked me. Those four shots of Patrón had me high as a kite. And all I wanted to do was lie down and get some much needed rest.

Before I realized it, I was out like a light.

When I woke up the following morning, it came with an excruciating migraine. There was no doubt in my mind that I had a hangover. Ugh! I hated those things. I should've reminded myself that that happens when you drink too much the night before. I also found myself lying on Nick's living room sofa with a warm blanket covering me. I heard Nick shuffling things around the kitchen so I called his name. "Nick, I'm in desperate need of some aspirins so my head can stop pounding," I yelled.

Nick peeped his head around the corner. "I've got some ibuprofen if that'll work."

"I'll take anything right now," I assured him.

A few minutes later, he walked out of the kitchen with a bottle of ibuprofen and a bottle of water and handed them both to me. "Thanks," I said and immediately ingested them both.

I saw Nick take a seat on the chair across from me before I laid my head back against the headrest of the sofa. I closed my eyes, believing this would help eliminate my headache faster. Boy, was I wrong.

"We're gonna have to come up with a really good alibi when the officers confront you and give you the news that your father is dead." Nick broke the ice.

"I know," I replied without opening my eyes. I wanted to pretend that everything around me was dark.

"Have you thought about what to tell 'em?" Nick wanted to know.

"Well, I know I can't say that I was home, especially after having that run-in with the fucking cops that pulled us over last night. That would be a dead giveaway. And who knows, they may even say that they smelled gasoline on you too," I pointed out.

"Don't worry about that. I'll deny it until my face turns blue. What we need to focus on is why we were in that parking lot and how long we were there."

I opened both of my eyes and looked directly at Nick. "Let's say that you picked me up to talk and thought that IHOP would be a good place to do it. But we never went inside because we started arguing."

Nick thought for a moment and then he said, "Okay, yeah, let's go with that. But if they try to put the heat on you, call Dylan's lawyer immediately. He'll keep those motherfuckers from interrogating you."

"What if I fuck up and say the wrong thing?"

"You gotta remain calm and you'll do good."

"You make that shit sound so easy."

"That's because it is."

I sucked my teeth. "I think I should just leave town for a little while until all of this blows over."

"Kira, you can't do that. Running away would make you a primary suspect. Just go home and act like nothing is wrong. And when the officers show up to your front door and tell you that they found your father's body, you gotta fall down to your knees and act like your world just fell apart. Shed some tears if you can. And if you know how to faint, then do that too, because those fuckers are gonna be watching you really close."

It took me several minutes to retain everything Nick said. And once my migraine subsided, it finally hit me that he was right. If I didn't go home, the cops would automatically suspect me of killing my father. So, what I've got to do now is build up enough gumption to leave Nick's apartment. I knew I would eventually have to face the cops, so why not get it over with and deal with whatever they bring my way. I was a smart girl, so I'd get through it.

Chapter 18

In the Nick of Time

Knots of anxiety filled up my entire stomach. Images of police officers parked outside my building or waiting at the front door of my apartment to arrest me as soon as they laid eyes on me, gave me more jitters. A few times I thought about turning my car around and leaving town. But then where would I go without a dime in my pocket? The majority of my money was stashed away inside of my apartment. The other small amounts of cash I had were in a couple of bank accounts I had around the city, which probably totaled up to about three grand. Now how far would that take me? No-fucking-where! My best bet was to go home like Nick said and act like everything was normal.

I chose not to have the valet park my car when I arrived at my apartment building. I decided to park my car on my own and keep my keys in my pocket, just in case I needed a clean getaway.

My heart beat faster with every step I took after I entered my building through the garage. It felt like I was being watched for some reason, but when I looked around no one was there.

"Come on, Kira, stop being paranoid. Just stay calm and every-thing will be all right," I mumbled underneath my breath.

I treaded lightly down the hallway of the floor where my apartment was located, but when I was about to make a sharp right turn, I heard voices. It stopped me in my tracks. It felt like I was coming unraveled at the seams.

I stood still for a second so I could hear what was going on and hopefully find out who could be behind those voices. "Will you open the door, already?" I heard a man's voice say.

"For some reason, the key seems like it doesn't want to work," I heard a woman reply. And from there, I knew it was Jimmy and his wife Molly Larson, a Caucasian, hippy couple that appeared to know everything about politics. They lived across the hall from me. They weren't a threat to me; however, I didn't want to run into them for fear that they'd ask me a bunch of fucking questions about everything that was going on with Dylan, my father, and myself.

Finally, after those two figured out how to open the door to their apartment, they went inside. Boy, was I relieved. A burst of energy revved up inside of me and sent me sprinting around the corner and down the hallway as fast as I could. And imme-diately after I got in front of my apartment door, I unlocked it, pushed it open, and was inside my place in less than ten sec-onds flat. After I closed the front door and locked it, I felt a lit-tle better.

The feeling didn't last long because as soon as I laid my keys down on the table in the entryway of my apartment, someone started ringing my doorbell. Panic-stricken, I stood still, won-dering who it was. I wanted to yell and ask who it was, but my mouth wouldn't open. I even wanted to walk to the front door to look through the peephole, but once again I was too afraid to move. I feared that if I moved my feet, the person at the front door would know that I was inside.

"Kira Wade, this is Detective Grimes. Are you in there?" the detective yelled out. Right then and there, my suspicions were proven correct. I stood there quietly on the verge of having a mini heart attack. My hands started sweating profusely while my mind tried to figure out what to do next.

Boom! Boom! Boom! Boom! The knocks grew louder and more frequent. "Ms. Wade, if you're in there, then I'm gonna need you to open the door," he belted out. Then I heard my neighbors' voices from across the hall.

"I don't think she's there," I heard Jimmy say.

"Yeah, it's been pretty quiet over there since you guys took her boyfriend to jail," Molly added.

"When was the last time you saw her?" Detective Grimes asked them.

"I haven't seen her for a couple of days now," Jimmy stated.

"Well, I saw her yesterday down in the lobby getting someone in valet to fetch her car," Molly replied.

"Do you remember what time that was?" His questions continued.

"I'm not sure. But I do know that it was sometime around six o'clock," Molly explained.

"Check with the guys in the valet. They use a daily log for all the residents in the building," Jimmy suggested.

"Thank you! I will do just that," Detective Grimes assured them.

"Hey, Detective, how's her dad doing?" Molly asked.

"He was murdered last night," I heard Detective Grimes say.

"Oh my God! Really?!" Molly blurted out first.

"You got to be kidding me, Detective," Jimmy added.

"No, I'm not. That's the reason why I'm here. To notify her."

"What happened?" Molly wanted to know.

"Yeah, what happened?" Jimmy interjected.

"I'm not at liberty to say right now. But watch the news. You'll find out then," Detective Grimes told them.

"Why don't you leave us your card and when we see Kira we'll give it to her and let her know that she needs to contact you," Jimmy suggested.

"All right, here you go," I heard the detective say, which indicated to me that he handed his card to my neighbors.

A few seconds later, everyone said their goodbyes and then it went completely quiet. I heard my neighbors' front door close, but that didn't mean that Detective Grimes had left the floor. And knowing that he was here to talk to me about my father spooked me. I knew one thing: It wouldn't be in my best interest to talk to that officer one-on-one. So, I knew that I had to lawyer up.

I stood there for a few more seconds just to make sure Detective Grimes was gone, but it seemed like as soon as I turned around to head down the hallway towards my bedroom, I heard a rustling sound at my front door. Startled by that sudden noise, my heart nearly burst through the cavity of my chest. I turned my head back around and saw a shadow moving under my door. I immediately stopped breathing. But when I saw a small white card slide underneath the front door I exhaled. It wasn't a sigh of relief but it was close enough.

I crept towards the front door, barely making a sound, and when I got close enough, I kneeled down and grabbed the card from the floor. Before looking at it, I crept away from the door as quietly as I could and headed into the kitchen.

While I held that detective's business card in my hand I noticed that there was something written on the other side. I turned the card over and read his note. *Ms. Wade, please call me immediately*. I wasn't fazed by his note because there was no way I was going to call him. I mean, was he crazy? Or was he on drugs to think that I would call him? I had nothing to say to that man. He had already threatened to lock me up and insinuated that he would throw away the key if he knew I had something to do with any of the murders that had taken place. What I would do, though, was get Dylan's attorney on the phone so he could give me the proper legal advice.

After I tossed the detective's business card on the countertop in my kitchen, I headed to my bedroom so I could take off my clothes and take a long, hot shower. Hopefully, by then, I'd have a clearer mind.

Chapter 19

My Baby Is Coming Home

I think I stayed in the shower for at least thirty minutes. My cue to turn the water off was when the water started getting cold. I tried to think about what my next step would be concerning my father's death, but I couldn't come to terms that I had murdered him. Did that make me a bad person? Or was that a wise choice I made? I figured, whatever the case was, I eliminated my father from ratting me out to the officers, sending Dylan to prison for a long time, and causing more problems by tying Kendrick and his boys to the murders of the judge, his wife, and Nancy. And now that I think about it even more, I did everybody a huge favor.

Immediately after I stepped into my bedroom I dried off, rubbed lotion all over my body, and then I slipped into a pair of boy shorts and one of Dylan's white T-shirts. I sure wished that he was here right now because I needed him to comfort me. I needed to be held by him, especially with everything going on. I guess my time with him will come soon enough.

I lay down on my bed with my cell phone in hand and wondered what I was going to say to Dylan's attorney once I got him on the phone. With all the murders committed, it wouldn't surprise me if my cell phone was tapped, which is why I knew

I needed to be very selective with my words. After mulling over how I was going to start the conversation, I finally got the gumption to dial his number.

When the line started ringing, my stomach filled up with knots. My heart started beating erratically when the phone rang for the third and fourth time. Then a woman finally answered. "Thanks for calling the law offices of Berlinsky, Moss and Fentress, how may I direct your call?"

"Hi, my name is Kira Wade and I was hoping I could speak with Mr. Berlinksy?" I replied.

"Can I ask the nature of this call?" the woman wanted to know.

"He represents my fiancé, Dylan Callender, so I need to run a few questions by him," I told her.

"Okay, well, let me find out if he's available," she said and then she put me on hold. I listened to the elevator music for about five seconds and then she returned to the line. "Hi, Ms. Wade, I'm back. I spoke with Mr. Berlinksy and he told me to tell you that he needs to see you, and would you be available to stop by the office in the next hour or so?"

"Did he say what it was for? I mean, is it about Dylan?" I wondered.

"No, I'm sorry, he didn't say," the woman replied.

"Can I speak to him for just a second?"

"He's on a conference call right now."

I let out a long sigh. "All right, let him know that I am on my way."

"Awesome. See you then."

It took me no time to get dressed. After I slid on a pair of sneakers, a pair of sweatpants, and a hoodie, I grabbed my car keys and my handbag and headed towards the front door. Be-

fore I opened it, I looked through the peephole to make sure
no one was standing on the other side of the door waiting for
me to come out. Once I noticed that the coast was clear, I
opened my front door as slowly and quietly as I could. Not
only was I trying to avoid running into Detective Grimes, I was
also trying to avoid seeing my nosy-ass neighbors Jimmy and
Molly. I refused to give them the satisfaction of smiling in my
face and laughing behind my back because of everything that's
been going on. I knew they would love to ask me a bunch of
questions about Dylan's situation. But that wouldn't happen,
not on my watch.

Everything seemed to be running smoothly after I slipped
out of my apartment and down the hallway towards the staircase; that is, until one of the maintenance guys that worked
and serviced my building opened the door that led the stairs. I
stumbled backwards. "Oh my God! You scared the crap out
of me!" I told him while I held my hand pressed against my
chest.

"I'm sorry, ma'am," he replied, and then he stepped to the
side, allowing me space to walk by him.

I looked at him, trying to jog my memory about where I'd seen
him before. He was a young black guy. He looked like he was in
his early twenties. I took a quick look at the name tag on his uniform and saw that his name was Mitchell. His name didn't ring a
bell so I figured that he was a new employee. And knowing that,
I knew that I was in no danger of being ratted on.

"It's okay," I finally said and then I made my way by him.

I pretended like I was going downstairs to another floor, but
the moment he closed the door to the staircase, I whirled my
body around and made a dash towards the door that led to the
parking garage. I opened the door slowly and peered around
the door. I scanned the entire area where my car was parked

and when I saw that there were six cars out there with no one in them, I stood up and sprinted across the garage floor until I got to my car. I fumbled with my keys a bit, but after I calmed myself down I was able to unlock the car door and climb inside.

I started the ignition without hesitation and as soon as I put my car in reverse, I turned my body slightly to the right to look over my shoulder and out the back window and nearly had a heart attack when I saw a man standing near the trunk of my car with a hoodie covering his head.

Once he figured out that saw him, he pulled the hoodie off his head, exposing his face. I blinked my eyes a couple of times to make sure I wasn't seeing things. But after that third time, I realized that the hood-wearing perpetrator was Kendrick. He stood there like he dared me to back my car into him. I kept my foot on the brake pedal and rolled down my passenger-side window. Seeing this, Kendrick walked slowly up to the car door, placed his elbows on the windowsill, and then he leaned his head in towards me.

"What's up?" I asked him. I was nervous as hell, but I refused to let him see it.

"I came by so we could talk," he said, his words barely audible. I watched him while he searched my face for a weak spot to suggest that he was intimidating me. I held my head up in a way to show him that I wasn't fazed by his presence.

"What we need to talk about?" I replied in a firm matter.

"We need to talk about your father," he said.

"What about him?" I replied quickly.

"Where is he? I haven't seen him around."

"I'm sure he's probably at home."

"Come on, Kira, don't play games with me," he hissed. He sounded like he was becoming annoyed.

"Kendrick, I promise you I'm not trying to play games. Just tell me what you want so I can get out of here." I gritted. I was losing patience. I was also losing time sitting here when I had more pressing matters to take care of.

"So, you're gonna sit there and act like you didn't set your pops on fire last night?" Kendrick replied sarcastically.

I swear, a lump instantly formed in my throat while my heart leaped from my chest. I became speechless. I didn't know whether to push him away from my car and drive away or jump out of the car myself and run away as fast as I could. Unfortunately for me, neither one of those choices would've been a good one, so I opened a small window of dialogue with him, but without incriminating myself. I got up the gumption to ask, "Kendrick, where are you going with this?"

"Let's just say that I know you and that nigga Nick's hands are dirty just like mine. And I must say that that was some gangsta shit. I didn't think you had it in you." He chuckled.

I sat there in silence, while he took this moment to laugh in my face.

"Oh yeah, I just saw that detective dude leaving your building not too long ago. So, did he break the bad news to you or did he accuse you of killing him?"

"I didn't give him a chance to talk to me. When he rang my doorbell, I ignored it," I explained.

"Well, you know he's gonna come back, right?"

"Yes, I know."

"Well, you better get your story together or you're gonna end up in a cell next to your man," Kendrick commented and then he let out a loud chuckle.

"Don't worry, I've got everything under control," I mentioned. By this time, I was getting sick of hearing his voice. And the fact that he was talking to me like I was a child didn't make the situation any better. This wasn't my first time having a run-in with the cops. I've been down this road a few times already, so I knew what I needed to do to stay a free woman.

"I'm sure you do," he said, but condescendingly, and then

he stood up and walked away from my car. I let out a sigh of relief after I saw him get into the passenger seat of a black, four-door Porsche truck. I couldn't see the driver because the windows were tinted. But I had a strong feeling that he had at least two to three guys in that SUV because Kendrick never travels alone.

I waited in the parking garage for a few minutes until I felt like Kendrick and his boys were long gone. Although he said that he knew Nick and I murdered my father, something in my gut told me that he didn't know for sure, which was why he was in my face fishing for answers. But then again, maybe he did know. Kendrick was a mysterious guy and he loved playing mind games when he could. It gave him a sense of power. But I say, to hell with him and his manipulative tactics. And if he continues to play this game with me, I will make sure I come out as the winner.

I finally drove out of the parking garage without running into anyone else. I went straight to Dylan's attorney's office, while I looked nervously over my shoulder and through my rearview mirror. I refused to let anyone else follow me, which meant I needed to be extra careful. Not only did my life depend on it, so did my freedom.

The drive to the attorney's office was pretty emotional. I couldn't get over the fact that Kendrick and Detective Grimes stopped by my place. Okay, I know it's Detective Grimes's job to harass me for answers that will solve the murder cases, but Kendrick was way out of line. Not too long ago he sent one of his henchmen into my building to threaten me while I was waiting by the elevator. I didn't even see that guy coming. He popped out of nowhere. And then today, Kendrick did the same thing. I had to draw a line in the sand, because this couldn't keep happening, especially with everything that's been going on. I knew one thing: If things didn't start turning around for the better, I was gonna have to get Nick and Dylan involved. As simple as that.

———◆———

"My name is Kira and I'm here to see Mr. Berlinsky," I said to a young white woman the moment I stepped up to the reception area.

"Great! So, while you're signing in, I'm gonna let Mr. Berlinsky know that you're here," she told me and then got up and disappeared into another part of the office. About a minute later, she reappeared and took a seat at her desk. "He'll be out here to see you in a couple of minutes," she assured me.

"Thank you," I replied and then I took a seat in the waiting area. I noticed I was the only one there, which was fine, but for some reason, I was beginning to feel alone. My father was dead and my boyfriend was in jail. So how could I correct this? How could I make my situation better? Right now, I was in a vulnerable place. If Dylan weren't in jail, none of this mess would be going on. Dylan was a fixer. He avoided a lot of things, but whenever his back was pushed against the wall, he'd get vicious. I loved that about him. It showed me that he wasn't a man that would be pushed around. Everyone on the streets knew him well. Kendrick was one of those people that knew how Dylan was. He hated Dylan but there was a level of respect on both sides, which brought me to a place about whether or not I should tell Dylan that Kendrick paid me a visit. Knowing how Dylan is, I knew he was going to flip out. Nothing good would come out of that. So maybe I should tell Nick instead. That way he could stow it away in the back of his mind and when the opportunity presented itself, he and Dylan could handle it.

While I thought about everything that was going on in my life, Mr. Berlinsky walked into the waiting room, smiled, and extended his hand, all while thanking me for coming by his office at such short notice.

"It's okay, I'm glad I stopped by because I needed to speak with you as well, but I wasn't comfortable with saying it over the phone," I explained.

"Well, come on back to my office," he instructed me, as he led the way.

Immediately after he and I sat down he said, "How are you feeling right now? Are you okay?"

Puzzled by his question, I hesitated for a second while I processed this question and then I said, "If you are referring to the fact that Dylan is still in jail, then no, I'm not okay."

"No, that's not what I'm talking about."

"Then what are you talking about?"

"I take it that you don't know," he said, and then he paused.

Watching his body movements and listening to every word he uttered, I knew then that he was talking about my father. But of course, I couldn't let on that I knew anything about it. If I did, and he found out later that I had not yet talked to any officers, I could become the number-one suspect. So again, I had to do this thing right. I had no room for errors. "Mr. Berlinsky, will you please tell me what you are talking about?" I finally said.

"Have any police officers or homicide detectives stopped by your house to talk to you today?" he asked.

"Detective Grimes stopped by my apartment not too long ago and slid his business card underneath my front door. He even put a note on the back of the card, saying that he needed me to call him. But I threw the business card in the trash. I will not allow him to continue harassing me. Those days are over."

"Listen, Kira, I don't know if I should be telling you this, but I feel obligated since I'm your fiancé's attorney—"

I cut him off in midsentence. "Feel obligated to tell me what?"

"It's being reported that your father was murdered last night. And whoever murdered him was trying to send a message."

Before I said another word, I knew I had to act like this was my first time hearing these words. I also knew that if I didn't put on a show as if my heart had just got ripped out of my chest, then Mr. Berlinsky would probably look at me in a different light. So for me to pull this off, I thought back to when my grandmother was murdered a few years back. I left Virginia because of her. In my mind, she was the only person that ever really loved me. Thinking about her instantly filled up my eyes with tears. "Please, tell me you're kidding? I just spoke with him yesterday and he was fine," I said as I began to sob.

Mr. Berlinksy grabbed a couple of Kleenex from the box on his desk and handed them to me. "I'm so sorry," he said.

"Are you sure? I mean, who told you this?" I flooded him with questions.

"I saw it on the news early this morning. And when I called down to the coroner's office, they confirmed it, since I'm representing someone whom he filed charges against."

"What happened to him? How did he die? And where is he now?"

"All I know is that they pulled them out of a burning SUV."

"No, don't tell me that! That can't be. I just spoke to him," I cried out.

Mr. Berlinsky stood up from his chair, walked around his desk, and then he wrapped his arms around my shoulders. "It's gonna be all right." He tried to console me.

I laid my head against his arm and cried like I was a newborn baby. "What am I going to do?" I asked him, while I began to wipe away the tears that saturated my face.

"Well, first of all, we're gonna have to get you some legal counsel, because if you don't call Detective Grimes back, either he or someone else is going to pressure you into going down to the precinct to interrogate you about your father's murder."

"Why would they do that? They know I loved my father." I continued to put on the act, while the tears continued to fall from my eyes. So far, I was doing a great job. Not only did I resemble a woman about to have a nervous breakdown, but I also got Mr. Berlinsky to suggest that I get legal counsel, without letting on that that was the reason why I had called him earlier. Everything was coming together perfectly.

"Don't take it personally. It's just a formality," he told me.

"Mr. Berlinsky, you know Detective Grimes hates my guts. If you recall, he thinks that I'm withholding information about the murders of Judge Mahoney and his wife. So, you know he's gonna try to make my life a living hell if he gets a chance to lock me up in a room with him," I said while I continued to sob.

"If you hire legal counsel then that won't happen. Whoever you choose to represent you will not allow a law officer to back you into a corner. So, let me make a call and see who I can get to help you," Mr. Berlinsky said and then he left my side. He walked back to the other side of his desk and reached for the office phone on his desk. I watched him as he dialed a number and put the phone up to his ear. By this time, I had toned down my sobbing. I also wiped my eyes with the Kleenex a few times when he'd glance at me. "Hey, Richard," he started off saying, "I've got a young woman in my office whose father was murdered last night and the detective who's assigned to that case wants to talk to her, but I advised her to seek legal counsel before she sits down with the guy. So, do you think you'll be able to help her?"

"Sure, I'll be glad to. Ask her how soon she would be able to stop by my office," I heard him say. The volume on Mr. Berlinsky's office phone was turned up pretty high. Before Mr. Berlinsky could repeat the other attorney's question, I nodded my head and whispered, "Where is his office?"

"His office is on the eighth floor of the Bank of America building on Waterside Drive," Mr. Berlinsky replied after he covered the receiver with the palm of his hand.

"Tell him I can be there in fifteen to twenty minutes," I continued to whisper.

Mr. Berlinksy removed the palm of his hand from the receiver and told the other attorney to be expecting me in the next fifteen minutes. After they both said their goodbyes, Mr. Berlinsky ended the call. Immediately after he hung up the phone, he looked at me and said, "I know this may not be a good time to say this, but now that your father is deceased, I can file a motion at the court clerk's office to have Dylan's case dismissed."

"Are you serious?" I asked, trying to give the impression that I was naïve.

"Yes, I am very serious."

"Does that mean he'll be getting out?"

"Yes, it docs."

"So how long does this take?"

"I'm going down to the clerk's office tomorrow morning. And when I'm done filing the motion, I'll give you a call," he assured me.

A few minutes later Mr. Berlinsky got up from his chair and walked me out to my car. He gave me some words of wisdom that made me feel somewhat better about what was going on. "Drive carefully," he told me, and then he waved me off as I exited the parking lot of his firm.

Chapter 20

I Need To Fix This

I drove away from Mr. Berlinsky's office with a half smile on my face. One part of me wanted to celebrate the fact that my fiancé, Dylan, was about to come home a free man. But the other part of me felt sad because I took my father's life to make it happen. Some people will look at me like I was a traitor, but realistically I didn't have any other choice. My father didn't think about the safety of my life, all he cared about was his judge friend and his wife. In my eyes, they meant more to him than I did. So, guess what? It was time to eliminate the toxicity that was plaguing my life.

I couldn't stop wondering how Dylan was going to feel once he found out that I took my father's life. He was a very protected man so I was sure he'd thank me, because my actions demonstrated how loyal I am to him. But then again, I was afraid that he would look at me differently.

Speaking of which, I started wondering why I haven't heard from him as of yet. Like clockwork, Dylan always called me every day between eight and nine a.m. He would do this right after breakfast was served at the county jail. And then he'd call me back, between eleven and twelve o'clock after the correctional officers serve the inmates' lunch. During these midday phone calls, he'd want to know what had I done since we talked. Since I stopped working at the dealership, I had started looking after my father more, until he started acting like a fake detective. And now that that's over, I wasn't too sure how I was going to fill that void.

———⋘•⋙———

Finding a parking space on Waterside Drive seemed nearly impossible. I had to circle the area five times before I found a place to park my car near the Bank of America building. It was time-consuming, but I had to do it because I refused to walk a mile to get to the building.

Immediately after I entered the Bank of America building, I hopped on the elevator and went up to the eighth floor. When the elevator door opened, I exited and followed the arrows that pointed in the direction of the attorney's office, which wasn't that far. As I walked up to the glass door, I noticed the attorney had his name inscribed in the middle of the glass. It read, RICHARD KESSLER, ESQ. ATTORNEY-AT-LAW. I entered the office and a receptionist greeted me. She was a Caucasian woman. She smiled and asked me how could she help me? I told her who I was and that I was there to see Mr. Kessler, and before she could respond Mr. Kessler walked into the reception area. He was a short, Caucasian man with good taste in tailor-made suits. Although he was completely bald, he was a very distinguished-looking gentleman. He kind of reminded me of George Clooney with no hair. He shook my hand and said, "You are a very pretty lady."

I gave him a half smile and thanked him. He instructed me to follow him back to his office, which was down a long hallway. As we walked, I peeked my head into all of the offices, from left to right. We finally arrived at the entryway of his office. "You can have a seat right here," he said, pointing to a leather chair opposite the chair that was behind his desk. I sat down and instantly looked around at all the awards and certificates he had framed and hung on the wall. To sum it up, his office was decorated just like Mr. Berlinsky's.

"So tell me, young lady, what's going on," he said after he sat down in his chair.

I thought for a moment so I could gather my thoughts and try to explain my situation without incriminating myself. Lawyers know when someone is lying to them. They can spot a liar a mile away. To keep it real, I was one of those liars, so I knew I had to sound convincing when I laid the cards down in front of this man.

When I felt like I was ready to talk I cleared my throat and started by saying, "I called Mr. Berlinsky's office to check on the status of my fiancé's case."

"What's your fiancé's name?" he interjected.

"Dylan Callender," I told him.

"Is he in jail right now?"

"Yes."

"What are his charges?"

"Well, what happened was he and my father got into a heated argument and one thing led to another. The result is that my father was accidentally shot and my fiancé was arrested and put in jail. He was given a bail hearing but the bail was denied because my father is a very influential retired judge. So, when the word circulated amongst his peers that my fiancé shot him, everyone banded together and made sure that he couldn't get out of jail."

"What's your father's name?"

"Judge Wade."

"Hey, wait a minute, that was your father that was murdered last night?"

I nodded my head the second Mr. Kessler reminded me of my father's demise. It was gut-wrenching to hear him utter those words from his mouth. And before I knew it, tears started falling from my eyes yet again. Mr. Kessler handed me a couple of Kleenex. "I'm sorry about your loss," he told me.

"I just can't believe that he's gone." I sobbed as a piercing feeling shot through my heart. The difference between the first time I cried and now had a lot to do with guilt. This feeling of guilt had also forced me to cry in front of Mr. Berlinsky.

"Does the homicide detective have any leads?" Mr. Kessler wanted to know.

"I'm not sure, and that's the reason why I am here. See, a detective named Grimes stopped by my apartment a few hours ago and slid his business card underneath my front door with a message scribbled on the opposite side asking me to give him a call."

"Do you have that business card with you now?"

"No, I left it at home. But I could go back there and get it if you want me to," I offered.

"That's not necessary, I know who he is. But let me ask you this—"

I sat there sobbing, waiting to hear Mr. Kessler's question.

"Have you ever had contact with this detective before?"

"Yes, several times. And each time I run into him, we never see eye to eye."

"Tell me about that."

"Well, he's investigating the murders of my father's friend and his wife, so out of the blue, my father convinces himself that he could assist with the investigation and starts feeding Detective Grimes false leads. One time my father told the detective that the same people that killed his friend and his friend's wife kidnapped him and that I knew who they were. I became livid when Detective Grimes questioned me about it. So, from that point, I told him to stop soliciting fraudulent information from my father, and then I told him to get lost."

"I'm assuming that didn't work."

"No, it didn't, which is why I need you as my voice."

"So wait, you think he's looking at you as a potential suspect?"

"I'm not sure. But I do know that he's got it out for me, so he won't be nice to me once we come face-to-face again. He may even start harassing me. And if that happens, I wanna be able to tell him to go straight to hell."

"No, no . . . no, you don't wanna tell him that. You could, however, let him know that if he wants to talk with you then he'd have to call me first so I could set it up. But please keep in mind that we're dealing with a homicide detective who's arrogant and overzealous. He knows the law like the back of his hands and he pushes the limits without crossing boundaries. And knowing his reputation, he won't stop at anything until he solves the case that he's harassing you about. So if there's anything I should know, tell me now so I won't be blindsided later on."

"Wait . . . you think I'm holding something back from you?"

"No, that's not what I'm saying. What I'm saying is, if there is something the homicide detectives know about, then I want to know about it as well so I can prepare a defense for you. Do you understand?"

"Yes, I understand," I replied and then I fell silent to jog my memory. To be perfectly candid, there were a lot of things I was holding back. But I couldn't open up and tell this guy because I knew I would expose all the lies I've told. I mean, let's be real. I was hiring him to keep the officers off my ass, but do you think he'd continue to shield me if he knew the whole truth? Hell no! So, guess what? I'm going to spoon-feed him like a newborn baby because no one is going to fully have my back but me.

"Is there anything else I need to know?"

I thought for a second longer and then I said, "The only other thing I think could be crucial is, while I was at Mr. Berlinsky's office he told me that since my father is now deceased, he's going to file a motion down at the courts to have the charges that my father filed against my fiancé dropped. And the backlash that's going to come from that will certainly have Detective Grimes thinking that either myself or my fiancé had something to do with his murder," I explained and without realizing it tears started falling from my eyes again.

"I agree," Mr. Kessler stated. "But, you did say that you didn't have anything to do with your father's murder, right?" Mr. Kessler added.

"Yes, Mr. Kessler, I had nothing to do with my father's murder," I said to him, even though I was lying through my teeth. Thankfully, the tears falling from my eyes gave the appearance that everything I had uttered from my mouth seemed plausible because otherwise, Mr. Kessler would've probably had his doubts.

Mr. Kessler began to watch me closely as I continued on with my act. A few times he made me feel like he was looking right through me. Then he'd change his posture by giving me a look of empathy like he genuinely cared about me and my situation and wanted to do everything within his power to make things better for me.

"Has anyone contacted you about coming down to the county morgue to ID your father's body?"

"No."

"Well, you're going to be getting that call pretty soon, so be ready."

"What if I don't get a call? Do you think it would be a good idea to go down to their office anyway?" I asked.

"Trust me, they will call you. And please be aware that Detective Grimes or another detective in his department may decide to pop up on you while you're there tying up loose ends concerning your father." He reached towards a stack of business cards on his desk. "Here," he continued as he handed me his business card. "If anyone approaches you in uniform or plain clothes carrying a badge, tell them you are not answering any questions without your attorney being present, and then I want you to give them my card and tell them to call me."

"Do you think that's gonna work?" I asked.

"Of course it is."

"What do you want me to do if they arrest me?"

"You said you had nothing to do with your father's murder, correct?"

"Correct."

"Well then, you have nothing to worry about. But if they try to detain you, I want you to call me immediately."

"Don't worry, I will."

"Do you have any questions for me?" Mr. Kessler wanted to know.

"How much is your retainer? And what will you charge me if things get ugly?"

"Since you haven't been charged with any crimes, my retainer will be twenty-five hundred dollars. After I receive that amount, I will make the necessary phone calls to let the authorities know that I represent you and that I will accompany you if and when they decide that they want to speak with you about their ongoing investigation. Now as far as my hourly rate, I charge three hundred dollars an hour. My receptionist will bill you at the end of every month," he explained.

"Do you have a credit card machine? Because I can pay you now with my debit card."

"My receptionist will take your payment in the reception area. So get with her before you leave the office and she will take care of the rest."

Feeling a sense of relief, I stood up from my chair and shook Mr. Kessler's hand. "I wanna thank you for putting my mind at ease."

"That's what I am here for."

"I guess, now I can concentrate on moving forward and mourn my father's death without the officers breathing down my neck."

"Yes, you can," he agreed.

I gave him a half smile, turned around, and I walked out of his office.

Chapter 21

Beyond My Control

I walked out of Attorney Kessler's office feeling a lot better than I did before I went inside. He made me feel like I could conquer anything that comes my way, especially now that his retainer was paid. I poked my chest out a little bit and raised my head high.

Immediately after I started up the ignition to my car and proceeded to leave, my cell phone started ringing. I looked down at the caller ID and noticed that my baby Dylan was calling me. At one point, I was happy that I was about to talk to him, but then I realized that a lot had happened to me in the last twenty-four hours and I wouldn't be able to talk about it over the phone because all phone calls from jail are heavily monitored and recorded. I went ahead and made the best of this situation.

"Hey, baby," I said in a low and sad tone.

"What's up with you? Why are you sounding like that?" he wanted to know.

"Baby, a lot is going on out here."

"Whatcha mean? Tell me what happened."

As bad as I wanted to tell Dylan what happened to my father, I knew I couldn't. In the cops' eyes, how could I know the details if they hadn't given me the news yet? There was no doubt in my mind that the jail was recording our conversation. So, whatever I wanted to say to Dylan, it better not have anything to do with my father's death, unless I wanted to incriminate myself. And since I didn't want to do that, I acted as if I had no knowledge of it. "Nothing happened, I'm just stressed out because my dad is worrying me to death. And you're not home to help me deal with it," I finally said.

"I take it that you and he had another argument about me?" Dylan stated as if he knew what was going on.

I sighed heavily, wanting to tell him that my dad was dead and that our troubles were long gone. But once again I had to remind myself that that subject was off-limits at this point. "No, I haven't talked to him in two days. And as bad as I wanna call him, I know he's gonna bring your name up, and then everything is gonna go downhill from there," I explained.

"Yeah, you're right. So, how are you doing otherwise?"

I sighed heavily. "Baby, I miss you so much. And I don't know how much longer I can take being out here by myself."

"Don't talk like that, Kira. Just hang in there. Everything is going to be okay. And when I get out of this fucking jail you and I are going to take a vacation somewhere on one of those small-ass islands in South America. A'ight?"

I let out another sigh. "Yeah, I guess," I said.

"When was the last time you talked to my moms and my sister?"

"That's a good question because I haven't spoken to either one of them in a couple of days," I told him.

"Well, I've called them both a couple of times and they never answer their phones. So, I want you to call them or go over there and check on them," he instructed me.

"Okay, I'll go. But the last time I went over there, Bruce answered the door, acting all weird and told me that your mother was asleep. So, I told him to tell her to call me when she gets up but she never did," I replied.

"Well, go over there again. And if that motherfucker gives you any problems, tell him he's gonna have to deal with me when I get out of here."

I let out another sigh and then I said, "Will do."

A few seconds later, Dylan switched topics and asked about his attorney. "Have you talked to him lately?"

"Yeah, I talked to him earlier," I replied nonchalantly.

"What was he talking about?"

"He told me that he's working hard to get you another appeal for a bail hearing."

"Fuck that bail hearing! I'm tired of wasting money on bail hearings. He needs to figure out another way to get me out of here. Your dad was shot by accident. And he needs to tell them that."

"Who needs to tell 'em?" I asked, feeling a bit confused.

"Kira, I'm talking about your pops," he corrected me. "Your pops needs to tell them what happened."

"Baby, can we please stop talking about that?" I pleaded. I wasn't in the mood to talk about my father. The feeling of guilt was taking over my entire body. I needed some relief so I pressured Dylan to talk about something else.

"Have you talked to Nick?" I asked.

"I called him right before I called you, but he didn't answer," Dylan replied. "Why? Have you talked to him?"

"Not since yesterday."

"What was he talking about?"

"Nothing. He just wanted to check on me to see if I needed anything."

"Well, if you talk to him before I do, tell 'im I tried to call him earlier."

"Okay," I said.

Dylan and I talked for the rest of the fifteen-minute call, and before our call was terminated, I reassured him that I loved him and that I had his back regardless of how the situation turned out. He thanked me but I could tell by the sound of his voice that he didn't think he was going to walk out of jail anytime soon. And at that very moment, I wished there was a way that I could make him feel differently. Telling him that he could be coming home any day now was at the forefront of my heart. But then, what would happen after I told him that? My guess was that he would start asking me a lot of questions. *How do you know that? Did my lawyer find a loophole in the case? Or is your father dropping the charges?* However things pop off, it wouldn't look good for Dylan or myself. So, I played smart and kept my mouth closed. I figured when the right time came, I'd be able to tell him everything.

Chapter 22

More News

Aside from the fact that guilt and shame were riding me, my emotions took a nosedive into the pit of my stomach when it dawned on me that I could spend the rest of my life in jail. Yes, I was free of the drama my dad brought on me with those murders, but now I'm feeling worse than I did when he was alive. Was I ever gonna get past this? Or was it going to haunt me for the rest of my fucking life?

While I cruised down Highway 195, it dawned on me that I didn't have anywhere to go. I couldn't go back to my apartment for the fear of running into Detective Grimes. Not to mention that my neighbors who lived across the hall from me would love to make a citizen's arrest. I could see those crackers calling the cops on me without blinking an eye. I couldn't have that, so I called Nick to see if I could chill out at his place for a few hours while I figured out my next move.

I used my Bluetooth device to dial his number. I pressed the speakerphone function after the call started ringing. To my surprise, Nick didn't answer his phone. It rang four times before the call went to voicemail. After I disconnected the line, I waited for a second or two and then I dialed his cell phone number again. This time the phone rang five times before it went to voicemail. "Hey, Nick, this is Kira. Where are you? I'm trying to come by your place and chill for a few hours. We also need to talk. So, call me back," I said and then I disconnected the call.

As I continued down Highway 195, it occurred to me that I needed to call Dylan's sister and mother back. Hopefully, they'd pick up and answer their phones this time.

I dialed Dylan's sister's cell phone number first. Unlike Nick's phone, Sonya's phone didn't ring at all. My call went straight to voicemail. *You reached the right person, but at the wrong time. Leave me a message at the sound of the beep.* BEEP!

I disconnected the call without leaving a message and redialed her cell phone number. For the second time, it didn't ring and it went straight to her voicemail. *You reached the right person, but at the wrong time. Leave me a message at the sound of the beep.* BEEP!

Frustrated, I pressed the END button and dialed Mrs. Daisy's phone number. I was relieved when her phone starting ringing. I was even happier after the call was answered. "Hello," I heard a man's voice say. I knew right off the bat the male's voice I heard was Mrs. Daisy's husband, Bruce.

"Bruce, Mrs. Daisy never called me back after I left you guys' house a couple of days ago. So, will you please put her on the phone so I can talk to her?"

"She's not here."

"Then where is she?"

"I don't know where she is. She left out of here over an hour ago with Sonya."

"Well, I just called Sonya's cell phone and it's going straight to voicemail."

"Maybe you should keep trying until she answers," he replied sarcastically.

"I will. Thanks," I said and disconnected the call. The sound of Bruce's voice made me cringe. He was such an evil-ass man. And for the life of me, I couldn't figure out why he was that way. I mean, Mrs. Daisy was a very kind and beautiful lady. She'd give anyone the shirt off her back. So, to have Bruce mistreating her the way that he did, made me want to set his ass on fire too.

Once again I was traveling down the highway, without a clue as to where I could go and hide out for a few hours. One part of me wanted to change my course and head out west where no one would ever find me. Then I remembered Nick telling me that leaving town wouldn't be such a good idea, especially now that my father had been murdered.

Mulling over the odds of the cops stalking my residence gave me an eerie feeling. If they were, then I was going to be in a shitload of trouble. But then, what if I was overreacting? Well, I figured the only way I'd find out is by going back to my apartment.

I decided to take the next exit and make a loop around to the other side of the highway and take the on-ramp to get back on the highway and head back in the direction I came from. I toyed with a few ideas of how I was going to act if Detective Grimes caught me going into my apartment building. If he walked up to me while I strolled through the lobby, I would hand him Mr. Kessler's business card and advise him to give him a call. But if he decided to wait outside of my apartment door and throw the handcuffs on me before I could get inside of my apartment, then I'd have to play it cool. I never allow cops to intimidate me.

Seven minutes into the drive heading back to my apartment, my cell phone started ringing again. Caught off guard by the sudden ring, I looked at the caller ID and noticed that the call was coming from Mrs. Daisy's cell phone number, so I answered it. "Hi, Mrs. Daisy," I said. But I got no reply. "Hello," I said once again after pressing the speakerphone button on my Bluetooth system. Still no response. "Hello, Mrs. Daisy, are you there?" I continued, and that's when I heard a little breathing on the other line. I remained quiet for a moment to see if I could hear some type of noise in the background but that didn't happen. Even the sound of breathing stopped. "Mrs. Daisy, are you there? Hello," I said once more. Sorry to say, I didn't get a response. What the caller did, though, was disconnect our call and the line went dead.

Immediately after the call ended I dialed Mrs. Daisy's cell phone number back. I waited for her phone line to ring but it went straight to voicemail, so I left her a voicemail message. "Mrs. Daisy, this is Kira. I saw that you just called me. I answered the phone but you didn't say anything. I figured maybe we were having a bad connection, so when you get a minute call me back," I said, and then I ended the call.

I got off at the Seventh Street exit and made a right turn on Brickell Avenue. Right after I made the turn a traffic cop flashed his lights and signaled for me to pull over to the side of the road. I swear, my heart felt like it was about to burst from my chest. "Where the fuck did this police officer come from? And why is he pulling me over?" I said to myself, simultaneously biting my bottom lip. I was a nervous wreck right now. I couldn't think straight even if someone paid me to, because all I could think about was why this man wanted me to pull my car over.

I watched him through my rearview mirror as he took his time to step out of his vehicle. At one point, I saw him speaking into the walkie-talkie device he had attached to his shoulder. One part of me wanted to pull off and start a highway police chase. But I decided against it because I knew that wouldn't be a smart thing to do. Who knows, I could end up causing a terrible car crash and I didn't want that, so I sat there and waited.

After waiting for a total of one minute and a half, the officer finally got out of his vehicle and approached my car. He was a very tall Caucasian man, so he had to stoop down a little bit so he could see my face.

"Officer, can you tell me why you pulled my car over?" I didn't hesitate to ask.

"Will you please hand me your license, registration, and insurance card?" he said, totally refusing to answer my question.

I grabbed my driver's license from my purse and then I took the registration and insurance card from the glove compartment and handed all three items to him.

"Remain in your car and I will be right back," he told me.

I sat in my car while anxiety slowly engulfed my entire body. For the life of me, I've always tried to do things the right way, but for some crazy reason, nothing good ever comes from it. I swear, it feels like someone has put a hex on me, because there's no way all of these bad things keep happening to me and I didn't initiate them. I didn't ask for Nancy, Judge Mahoney, and his wife to be murdered. And if my father would have minded his business, I wouldn't have sealed his fate.

All of the people that I just mentioned would be alive right now if they would've made better decisions. I guess what they say is true, "You reap what you sow."

I believe I looked at the traffic cop through my rearview mirror at least a dozen times, wondering what the hell he was doing in his car. Unfortunately for me, I got my answer sooner than I had anticipated when I noticed another patrol car pull up and park their vehicle directly behind the officer that I handed my driver's license to. The uniformed officer stepped out of his vehicle while the other traffic cop did the same. And instantly, my heart started beating at an unprecedented speed, all while I was still having the anxiety attack. Seconds later, I felt like I was paralyzed from the neck down. The only thing that seemed to be working on my body was my mind. And even that wasn't working properly. Every thought I tried to hold on to disappeared before I could make sense of it. I figured the only thing I could do now was take whatever came my way and deal with it.

Once I conditioned my mind to take whatever was coming my way, I took a deep breath and then I exhaled. I began to give myself a pep talk. "Come on, Kira, don't let these officers intimidate you. Just let these bastards know that if they want to talk to you, then they're gonna have to contact your attorney first."

"Excuse me, ma'am, but you're gonna have to step out of your vehicle," instructed the officer who had my driver's license.

"Am I being arrested?" I asked. I needed to know what was going on.

"Should I be arresting you?" the officer replied sarcastically.

"Will you just answer my question?" I huffed.

"Ma'am, we're only gonna tell you one more time to exit the vehicle," the other officer warned me.

"And what are you going to do if I don't?" My questions continued.

"Ms. Wade, don't give these officers a hard time. Just do what they say," I heard a male's voice say. Startled by this familiar voice, I turned my head around towards the passenger side of my car and saw Detective Grimes leaning his head slightly into the passenger-side window. He had this grimace-like expression on his face and that made me cringe instantly.

"I should've known you were lurking around one of these corners like a fucking crackhead," I hissed. I was freaking livid that these wannabe-ass patrol cops had me pulled over on the side of the road like I committed a crime. Well, I had, but they didn't know it.

"Desperate times call for desperate measures. So, come on and get out of the car so we can head down to the precinct."

"Are you arresting me?" I asked Detective Grimes.

"Not at this moment, but I'm very confident that it will only be a matter of time before I find something on you," he responded arrogantly, smiling the entire time.

"Look, I have an attorney and he said that I am not to talk to you without him being present," I told all three men standing there.

"Who is your attorney?"

"Mr. Kessler," I said with confidence.

"Oh, okay, well, step out of the vehicle and then we will allow you to call Mr. Kessler so you can tell him to meet us down at the precinct," Detective Grimes insisted.

Before I could utter another word, the officer that had my driver's license opened up the driver-side door and waited for me to step out of the car. I couldn't think of a word to describe how angry I was at that very moment. I mean, what kind of games were these guys playing? I was sick of these idiots harassing me. When would everybody leave me alone?

Finally, after going back and forth with the officers, I stepped out of my car with my purse in hand and stepped to the side so the other cop could close my car door. "Kira, give one of the officers your purse," Detective Grimes instructed as he walked around the hood of my car.

"For what? You said I wasn't under arrest," I huffed. These guys were irritating the crap out of me. "You know what? I'm calling my attorney right now," I warned them as I reached inside of my handbag. Before I could retrieve my cell phone, both traffic cops grabbed me and pinned me against the back door of my car. Detective Grimes snatched my purse from my hands. "Get off me," I yelled. I felt violated with these two cops manhandling me like I was a two-hundred-pound man.

"Stop resisting," Detective Grimes instructed me as he stood over top of me and the other two officers.

"Tell them to get off me," I snapped, struggling to get both officers to loosen their grip from my arms.

"We're not letting you go until you calm down," one of the officers said while twisting my arms with tremendous pressure.

"I'll calm down when y'all let me go!" I roared, while still resisting.

"No, you're gonna stop moving before we throw handcuffs on you." Detective Grimes threatened me. "You know you're making things harder than they're supposed to be. I mean, all you have to do is stop resisting."

"Why don't you tell these rookie-ass cops to stop twisting my fucking arm, they're hurting me!" My voice boomed.

"Fuck it! Throw the cuffs on her and put her ass in the back of the squad car!" Detective Grimes demanded.

"Throw the cuffs on me for what? You said I wasn't being arrested!" I yelled and screamed while I was trying to break away from them.

Before I could blink my eyes, Detective Grimes and the other two officers' bodies slammed me down to the ground, burying my face in the gravel scattered off to the side of the road. One of the officers applied pressure to my back with one of his knees, all to place the handcuffs around my wrist. "You fucking lied to me! You said that I wasn't being arrested and that I could call my lawyer!" I snapped.

By this time, the tears from my eyes covered my entire face. I couldn't believe that I was being treated like a fucking animal. They hog-tied my wrists and ankles and threw me in the back of the police car. I was lying on my stomach screaming frantically at these assholes about how I was going to sue the whole Miami-Dade Police Department. "I am going to make sure that all three of you clowns lose your fucking jobs because of this."

"Good luck with that!" Detective Grimes responded humorously, while he looked back at me from the front passenger seat. "Come on, Sanchez, let's get out of here," he continued after he turned back around to face forward in his seat.

"So, you're gonna make me lie down on my stomach the entire drive to the police station?"

"You left us no choice," he answered without looking back at me.

"That's bullshit and you know it," I barked, trying to hold my head up.

"Believe me, you have far more important things to worry about than lying on your stomach on the ride back to the precinct," he commented.

"What important things are you talking about?" I asked him.

"You'll find out soon enough."

What kind of answer was that? Was he trying to corner me with that comment? I needed to know what the hell he was talking about. Was he talking about my father? Did he have the evidence that I murdered him? If he did, then why hadn't he mentioned it? Was he setting me up so I could tell on myself? Well, if that was the case then he could forget it. I would never tell on myself. That would be the most foolish thing I could ever do. I mean, who commits a crime and then turns themselves over to the cops? No one I know. So, I figured whatever Detective Grimes was talking about could not possibly have anything to do with me. I guess now would be a good time to tell him to go and fuck himself. Better yet, I'd just let Mr. Kessler handle his stupid ass.

Speaking of which, I wasn't exaggerating when I told Mr. Kessler that this man had it in for me. He wanted me to suffer because I wouldn't help him solve his murder cases. But he didn't realize that the people that murdered Judge Mahoney, his wife, and Nancy weren't to be messed with. As soon as they found out that I helped Detective Grimes, they would kill me and everyone I loved or cared about. Kendrick and his boys were known for killing snitches and guys who'd try to rob his stash houses. I wasn't going to give Kendrick a reason to murder me. Not in this lifetime. No way! I learned a long time ago that when you learn to pick and choose your battles, you'll live with less stress and you'll live a lot longer.

During the rest of the drive to the police precinct, I didn't say another word to Detective Grimes. I refused to give him the satisfaction that he was breaking me down. Instead, I laid my head down on the back seat and closed my eyes for a moment.

Chapter 23

What Happens Next?

Upon arrival at the precinct, Detective Grimes and the other police officer that was driving grabbed me and dragged me out of the back seat. They were using unnecessary force, so I snapped on them again. "Why the fuck are y'all handling me like this? I can walk, so take these plastic-ass zip ties off me," I yelled.

"If you don't shut up, I will make sure that you wear these zip ties for the next twenty-four hours."

"You can't do that!" I yelled once more. "You are violating my civil rights. My attorney is going to have you begging for your fucking job after all of this is over!" I warned him.

Unfortunately for me, my threats fell on deaf ears. Detective Grimes and all of the other police officers stood around and smiled at me like I was a fucking joke. "So, y'all think this is funny, huh? Keep laughing and I'm going to have your jobs too!" I roared.

"Put her in interview room 2," a plainclothes officer told Detective Grimes.

"Roger that," Detective Grimes replied.

Interview room 2 was only a few feet away, so it only took Detective Grimes and the other police officer thirty seconds to carry me into the room and untie me. Shortly thereafter, they placed me in the chair with a table in front of me. There was another chair on the opposite side of the table. It didn't take long for me to figure out that that chair was going to be for Detective Grimes or some other detective while they're on their quest to interrogate me. In my mind, it didn't matter who'd end up sitting there. I was going to remain tight-lipped until my attorney arrived anyway.

As Detective Grimes and other officers walked towards the door, I asked them when they would allow me to call my attorney.

Detective Grimes slightly turned his head towards me and replied, "I'm gonna work on that now."

"Well, can I use the bathroom?" My questions continued.

"I'll get a female officer to assist you in just a few minutes," he said and then he exited the room.

I sat there quietly for a few minutes. It was a total of thirty minutes to be exact and there was not a female police officer in sight. So, at that moment, I stood up from the chair, walked to the door, and started knocking on it. "I need to use the restroom," I yelled from my side of the door. And, of course, no one responded. So, I started knocking on the door again. "I know you can hear me. I said I need to use the restroom!" I yelled. But once again, no one responded or even acknowledged that I had even said anything.

This made me angry, and that's when I started kicking and banging on the door. "I know y'all hear me! I said I need to use the restroom. I'm gonna piss on myself if you don't let me out of here," I snapped.

Finally, after threatening to urinate on the floor in that interrogation room, someone decided to open the door. I took two steps to the left, to give the person enough room so they could open the door. "I'm gonna take you to the restroom, but don't kick the door like that again," the female officer said. She was an average height and size, black female officer with what seemed like a chip on her shoulder. "I'm ready to go to the restroom now," I said, totally ignoring her sarcasm.

"Let's go." she said, and then she escorted me out of the room.

I walked a few feet ahead of her and glanced around the entire room made up of cubicles. I saw a few plainclothes detectives. And I also saw a few uniformed officers sitting in their assigned cubicles while the other ones walked around like they were working.

"The bathroom is right down the hall on your left," the female officer told me as she pointed in that direction. When we reached the door of the restroom she said, "I'm gonna stand right here and wait for you, so don't try anything stupid."

I frowned at her and replied, "Why are you acting like I was arrested?"

"Because you were," she said.

"Whatcha mean, I was arrested? I didn't do anything. I was driving down the street in my car and minding my own business when your colleagues pulled me over. So how could I have been arrested for doing that?" I questioned her.

"I'm afraid that you're going to have to ask Detective Grimes about that."

"Where is he?" I asked while I stood toe-to-toe with the female officer.

"He stepped out for a moment but he will be back very soon."

"See, this is bullshit! How can I get arrested when I haven't done anything?" I snapped.

"Listen, if you don't go and use the restroom right now, I will take you back to the interrogation room," she warned me.

"I'm gonna go in there, but when are y'all gonna let me call my lawyer?"

"If you act like you have some sense, then I'll let you call your attorney when you come out of the bathroom," the officer promised me.

Feelings of relief started building up inside of me. I knew I wasn't out of the woods yet, but if I played my cards right, I could call my lawyer and have him shut this whole precinct down.

Without further hesitation, I went inside the restroom, used it, washed my hands, and came right back out. The female officer was waiting there at the door like she said she would. "You're still gonna let me call my lawyer now, right?" I asked.

"Yeah, so walk over to that single chair by the phone on the wall," she replied while pointing to a wooden chair placed directly underneath what looked like a pay phone.

"Am I gonna have to call my lawyer collect?" I wanted to know.

"No. Just press the numbers 1 and 9 and that will give you a dial tone. And once you hear it, you'll be able to call your attorney."

As I was instructed, I pressed the numbers and then I dialed the number to my attorney's office. Mr. Kessler's receptionist answered the phone on the second ring. "Thanks for calling Attorney David Kessler's office. This is Megan speaking; now how may I help you?" she asked.

"Hi, Megan, my name is Kira Wade. I just left the office like an hour ago and paid you the retainer fee for Mr. Kessler."

"Yes, I remember, how can I help you?"

"Is Mr. Kessler still in his office?"

"Yes, he is, but he's on a conference call at the moment. But if you tell me what you need, I may be able to help you."

"Megan, I am in police custody. And I need you to let Mr. Kessler know that I was pulled over on the side of the road for nothing. Then I was hog-tied and dragged into this police precinct and was just told by one of the female officers that

I've been charged with a crime but she's not sure what it is. So, I need Mr. Kessler to get down here ASAP."

"Which precinct are you being detained at?" Megan asked me.

"I'm at the West District Station on 142nd Avenue."

"Do you know the name of the arresting officer?" Megan's questions continued.

"It was Detective Grimes," I said, and then my attention drifted away from the conversation I was having with Megan. I heard her mumbling something, but I couldn't repeat one word she just uttered. I became instantly distracted after I noticed Detective Grimes sitting in another interview room only twenty feet away from where I was, having a fucking conversation with Nick. Now this explained why he hadn't answered his cell phone when I called him.

From experience, before detectives start an interrogation, they always close the door to that room so the informant or person of interest would feel that privacy factor, which leaves me to believe that Detective Grimes kept that door slightly ajar so I could see Nick. He planned this move. My question now was, how long had Nick been here and what had he told Detective Grimes?

"Has he tried to interrogate you or ask you any questions?"

"Nick, what are you doing in there?" I murmured.

"I'm sorry, Kira, but did you say something?" Megan asked me.

"No, I wasn't talking to you," I replied while I watched Nick closely. "Megan, I've got to go. Just tell Mr. Kessler to get down here as soon as possible." I ended the call.

I sat there quietly, trying to remember all the incidents that I've seen Nick get into with Dylan and a few other guys, and I can't remember one time where Nick snitched. Nick has always been a straight shooter about everything. He has always been trustworthy too. Dylan has never said one bad thing about Nick. In fact, Dylan has said over a dozen times how Nick would lay down his life for him. That's how close they were. But as I sat here and watched Nick's body language, I was beginning to see a different person. Nick seemed to be engaged in a heavy conversation with Detective Grimes. I even heard Nick laugh a few times too. So, what's going on? Is he in that freaking room smiling in that cop's face or am I seeing things? I thought to myself while my blood boiled inside of me. Then it hit me like a ton of bricks that Nick was in there trying to save his ass. Was he in there snitching and pinning the murder of my father on me? What a fucking traitor and a bitch! Wait until I tell Dylan. He was going to have Nick's head when all of this was over.

After sitting there for a couple of minutes, the female officer approached me. "Are you done using the phone?" she asked me.

"Yes, I'm done," I replied and stood up.

"Well, let's go," she said.

Immediately after we started walking back in the direction of the interview room, Detective Grimes said something to Nick and instantly Nick whipped his head around and looked directly at me. He looked at me like he'd seen a ghost. Words could not explain the devastation I was feeling right now so I put my head down and continued to walk towards interrogation room 2.

I sat down in the chair while the female officer closed the door and locked it. I laid my head down on the table in front of me and wondered what had just happened.

Hundreds of questions and assumptions scrambled around in my head, but none of them made any sense. But what stuck out in my head more so than anything was how Nick looked at me when he saw me. Was that the face of a guilty man? A traitor? A snitch? Whatever it was, I saw it with my own eyes.

While all of these thoughts began consuming me, knots started forming in the pit of my stomach and I felt a massive headache approaching. The feeling of not knowing started riding me like the saddle on a horse. To put it plainly, it felt like I was about to have a nervous breakdown. And the fucked up part about it was that I was suffering all of this pressure on my own.

"Dylan, baby! Where are you when I need you?" I mumbled under my breath. I needed my fiancé here with me more than I had at any other time.

I sat in the room for at least another thirty minutes before someone knocked on the door and walked in. I lifted my head from the table and turned around only to see Detective Grimes walk into the room. He had another detective accompany him. "Kira, this is Detective Mann. He will be sitting in on our interview," Detective Grimes said, and then he closed the door to the room. Detective Mann stood alongside him.

"What fucking interview? Didn't Nick tell you everything you need to know?" I replied sarcastically.

"He told me enough."

"So, then why are we having this conversation?"

"Because I wanna give you a chance to come clean with me. If you help me then I'll be able to help you."

"Help you how?" I hissed. "You don't give a fuck about me. All you want is for me to be your snitch just like you made my father."

"That's funny you mention that . . ." Detective Grimes said and then he paused.

"Listen, Detective, my attorney will be here in a few minutes, so I don't have anything else to say to you."

"Kira, you don't have to say another word. But I have to inform you that your father was murdered last night," he finally said, watching my facial expression and body language the entire time.

There I was, sitting down in front of these two men watching me like a fucking hawk, so how was I supposed to react? What was I supposed to say? I knew I was supposed to act surprised, but would it work? I mean, Detective Grimes just got through talking with Nick, so were these two trying to railroad me into a confession, or what?

"That's bullshit!" I replied, trying to downplay his statement.

"Stop trying to blow smoke up my ass! You know I know that you had something to do with your father's murder!" he accused me after he took a few steps towards me.

"My father isn't dead. So, stop saying that!" I shouted.

"Cut it out! Nick already told us everything."

Before I could utter another word, the door opened, and in came Mr. Kessler. I was so freaking happy to see him. I stood up to my feet and tried to embrace him, but Detective Grimes grabbed me by the arm. "You need to have a seat!" he ordered me.

I snatched my arm away from him. "Keep your damn hands off me, you fucking fake-ass Robocop!"

Detective Grimes reached out to grab me again but Mr. Kessler forced his way between us. "Detective Grimes, if you wanna stay working on the police force, you better learn how to control yourself," Mr. Kessler interjected.

Detective Grimes turned his attention towards me and then he looked back at Mr. Kessler. "I'm gonna bury your ass before all of this is over!" he threatened.

"Have you charged my client with any crime?" Mr. Kessler asked both detectives.

Detective Grimes hesitated for a brief moment and then he said, "No."

"So, why did that female officer tell me that I had been arrested?" I huffed. I was getting more pissed off by the second.

"Who told you that?" Grimes asked.

"Don't play dumb with me. You know who told me."

"Listen, Kira, we only brought you in so we could ask you where you were last night between the hours of eight and eleven p.m."

"Don't answer that," Mr. Kessler instructed me.

"Why won't you allow her to answer the question?"

"Because I have not had a chance to brief her. Now if you'll excuse us," Mr. Kessler replied and then he escorted me out of that interview room. I watched Detective Grimes from my peripheral vision and I could tell from his facial expression that he was livid that Mr. Kessler whisked me out of there. He thought he had me backed into a corner. But thanks to my attorney for rescuing me.

While Mr. Kessler and I were heading towards the exit door, I remembered that the officers had my car. "Hey wait, they have my car and my car keys and I can't leave here until I get 'em."

"Okay, stay right here and I'll be right back," he told me and then he walked back to the department where the homicide detectives were. I took a seat on a bench in the lobby area of the precinct. I closed my eyes and leaned my head back against the wall. Thoughts of Nick talking to Detective Grimes had me on edge. For the life of me, I couldn't figure out why Nick would sit down and kick it with Detective Grimes like they were fucking cool or something. Did he know that he screwed up the loyalty factor? If he didn't, then he'd better do some soul searching, because once I got a chance to talk to Dylan about this, things between Nick and Dylan were going to get extremely ugly.

Mr. Kessler returned approximately five minutes later. He had my keys in hand and a document with the information of the make, the year, and the model on it. "Here are your keys. They have your vehicle at the city impound. Come on, I'll drop you off," he said, and then we left.

On our way to the city impound, Mr. Kessler gave me a laundry list of things to do moving forward. "After you pick up your vehicle, I want you to go down to the county morgue so you can ID your father's body. Then I want you to go home and call a bug device specialist so they can scan your house for any surveillance devices or cameras. I can't have you walking around your apartment talking freely while the detectives can hear everything you say."

"Isn't that against the law?" I questioned Mr. Kessler.

"If the county detectives have probable cause, then they could get the judge to sign off on it," he explained.

"That's total bullshit!" I spat.

"Yes, it is, so that's why I'm going to need you to do everything I tell you to do. We can't have any mix-ups. Understood?"

I nodded my head.

After Mr. Kessler pulled up to the gate of the city impound, I sat in his car for a brief moment trying to figure out how I should handle the situation with Nick. "Is there something wrong?" he wanted to know.

"I saw Detective Grimes interviewing my fiancé's best friend while I was using the phone to call you."

"What's his name? And how close is he to your fiancé?"

"His name is Nick. And he and my fiancé sort of grew up together."

"Why do you think Detective Grimes interviewed him?"

"I'm not sure," I lied. I couldn't tell him that Nick was with me on the night I murdered my father. If I did that, I might as well have made the confession to the cops.

"Do you think it had something to do with your fiancé shooting your father?"

"I'm not sure, but I will find out."

"Oh no, you don't want to do that. Detective Grimes may have gotten him to cooperate. Who knows, he may be the one that murdered your father."

"I don't think he's that type of guy," I said, and then I reached for the door handle and opened the passenger-side door.

"You never know. But anyway, if you need anything, I'm just a phone call away."

"Thank you," I said and then I got out of his car. I went inside of the city impound business office and got the woman behind the counter to assist me. I gave her the document Mr. Kessler gave me and after I paid her a hundred and fifty dollars, she escorted me onto the grounds to retrieve my car, and then she opened the gate so I could drive out of there.

As badly as I wanted to call Nick and curse him out, I decided that it wouldn't be a smart move, since my attorney said that it wouldn't be a good idea. More importantly, he was a snitch now, so I figured the best thing for me to do was travel in the opposite direction of him. At least until Dylan got home and took care of this situation.

Chapter 24

Beyond My Control

The county morgue was only a few streets away from the city impound, so it didn't take me that long to get there. The moment I stepped foot out of my car, I noticed that my hands had started sweating and my heart rate picked up speed. From there I knew I was about to have an anxiety attack. "Come on, Kira, you can handle it," I uttered to myself.

I took a couple of deep breaths, exhaled, and then I went inside the building. At the help desk was an elderly white woman waiting to assist me. She smiled as I approached her. "Good evening, can I help you?" she asked me.

"Yes, ma'am, I need to go to the morgue," I told her.

"You mean the coroner's office?" she corrected me.

"Yes, ma'am."

"Well, if you go down this hallway, make a right turn at the first corner, there is a set of elevators. Take one down to the ground floor, and as soon as you get off the elevator the office will be on your left."

I smiled and thanked her and then I headed towards the elevator.

The elevator ride down to the ground floor was a bit shaky.

It felt old and raggedy. It even made loud noises while it was moving. Thank God the ride wasn't that long because otherwise, I would've regurgitated everything I ate for breakfast.

Immediately after I got off the elevator, I walked into the coroner's offices but no one was there to greet me. There were two desks and two chairs in the waiting area, but again there was no one in sight. "Excuse me, is there someone here?" I yelled, hoping this would get someone's attention. And it worked. I heard a door open and close and then I heard footsteps. Seconds later, a middle-aged white man came from around the corner and greeted me. He was wearing scrubs, a white jacket, and a pair of Crocs on his feet. He extended his hand to me and introduced himself. "Hi, my name is Brad. How can I help you?"

"I was told by the officers that I needed to come down here to ID my father's body."

"When was your father brought in?"

"I'm assuming it was yesterday or earlier this morning."

"How was your father killed?"

"I was told that he was burned inside of a car," I explained.

"Okay, well, follow me," he said, and then he turned around and started walking back in the direction he had come from initially.

I followed him down the hallway and through a metal door. The metal door led to a cold room with four dead bodies lying on tables with white sheets covering them. The sight of these dead people made me feel uneasy. "Why is it so cold in here?" I complained. In hindsight, I was trying to find a reason to leave out of here before the coroner got a chance to show me my father's lifeless body.

"I'm sorry about that. But the room has to be a certain temperature while I perform the autopsy."

"Well, will you just show me where my dad is so I can leave? I'm sorry, but this room is creeping me out."

"Sure, he's over here," the coroner said as he pointed to the fourth body on the end.

As he began to pull the sheet back from my father's face, I saw how his body was charred to the top of his head, and immediately turned my head. "No, I'm sorry but I can't do this," I said and was instantly brought to tears.

"I am so sorry, ma'am," the coroner apologized.

"No, is not your fault. You didn't know," I replied while I sobbed.

Brad walked over to my side and placed his arm around me as if he was trying to comfort me. "Let me escort you back to the front office," he insisted.

After we arrived back at the front office, he handed me a few documents to sign. The first document I signed gave the coroner permission to perform my father's autopsy. And the second document I signed stated my father's full name, date of birth, home address, and that I was his next of kin, so I will be responsible for moving his body after the autopsy has been performed. Once everything was established between the coroner and me, I got out of there as quick as I could.

<hr>

The moment after I got into my car to head home, a mountain of emotions consumed me. I sat there in the driver's seat of my car and let out a floodgate of tears. Then I started punching the steering wheel over and over. "Why, Daddy? Why? Why couldn't you just leave shit alone?" I screamed while trying to block out the image of the top of his charred head.

"Daddy, this didn't have to happen," I sobbed.

At that very moment, I felt like a monster. I felt like a cold-hearted bitch. The thought of my deceased mother and grandmother looking down at me, and what I did, made me feel heartless.

How did I turn into this callous person? I remember once

upon a time when I was a good girl. A church-going girl that made straight A's throughout school. I was also my father's little bratty girl. A daddy's girl! He used to do everything with me. Ride our bikes together. Play toss and catch. Hide-and-seek. You name it, my father and I did it. So to stoop down to the level where I had to murder him to save myself was gut-wrenching. When would the bloodshed stop? I hoped and prayed that it ended here because I couldn't take the news of another person getting murdered. I was done.

I wasted little time driving back to my apartment. I figured since I didn't have anywhere else to go, going home would suit me just fine. I mean, it's not like I had to hide from Detective Grimes anymore. He saw me, he said what he had to say, and now I could go home in peace.

When I pulled up to my building, I started to have one of the valet guys park my car, but I changed my mind at the last minute and drove into the parking garage on my own. I wasn't in the mood to see any of my neighbors or any of the people that worked in my building. I refused to give anyone the pleasure of laughing in my face. Not today. Not ever.

Thankfully, after I parked my car in the garage, no one was around. I rushed onto the elevator and pressed the number to my floor. After the bell rang and the door opened, I scurried onto my floor and made a beeline to my apartment. As luck would have it though, I couldn't get into my apartment without someone seeing me.

While I was unlocking the front door to my apartment, my neighbor Molly stuck her nosy-ass head out her door. "Hey, Kira, how are you?" she asked, in an annoying way.

"I'm fine. Thanks for asking," I said, while I continued to unlock the door with the key to my apartment, which of course seemed like it didn't want to work.

"I'm sorry about your loss. A detective came by your place looking for you earlier so he could give you the news. Unfortunately, you didn't answer your door, so he left his card with Jimmy and me," she explained while my back was still facing her.

"I've already talked to him," I replied as I continued to jiggle the front door key into the lock. Finally, after forcing my key to fit in the lock properly, I got it to turn, and then my front door magically opened.

"Well, if you need anything I'm just across the hallway," she yelled out while I was closing my front door.

"Nosy bitch!" I hissed as I locked the door.

I threw my handbag and car keys onto the coffee table in my living room and then I headed down the hallway to my bedroom. When I entered my bedroom, I marched towards my walk-in closet and before I could get within a few feet of it, I saw the shadow of a man coming up from behind me. My heart nearly burst through my chest cavity, which meant that I was about to fight for my life. So, when I turned around to defend myself from what was about to happen next, I was yanked up in the air with a mighty force. My feet were dangling in the air. And right before I bellowed out a scream, my mouth was covered with a huge hand. My yell for help was muffled. From where I was standing, I was at a disadvantage. Everything went fast after I went into defense mode. I jerked my body back and forth while I kicked my feet hysterically. "Stop fighting, Kira. It's me, Nick," a male's voice whispered in my ear.

I continued to kick and resist the guy because I knew Nick wouldn't hold me the way this guy was. And why was he covering my mouth with his hand? Nick wouldn't do that either. "Kira, I need you to calm down and I'll let you go." The guy tried reasoning with me.

After I heard the guy's voice for the second time, it registered in my head that it was Nick, so I finally stopped resisting him. And the moment he let me go, I turned around and faced him. "What the fuck are you doing in my house? And how in the hell did you get in here?" I huffed. I couldn't believe that this snitch had the balls to stand in front of me after what he did earlier down at the precinct.

He pressed his pointer finger against his lips and shushed me. He leaned in towards me and whispered into my ear, "I think your apartment is bugged."

I pushed him back away from me. "Why are you here?" I whispered back.

"Give me something to write with." He continued whispering.

I stepped away from him and walked out of my bedroom. Nick followed me to the kitchen, and when I grabbed a legal pad of paper and an ink pen from one of the kitchen drawers, I handed them both to him. He took both items and placed the notepad on the countertop. He held the ink pen in his hand and started writing. He wrote a very quick note and then he slid the legal pad in my direction. The note read, *We need to talk. But we can't do it here.*

I took the pen from his hand and wrote a reply. *Why the fuck do we need to talk? Didn't you say enough to that fucking cop you were laughing with earlier?*

Nick shook his head and grabbed the ink pen back from me. *The only reason why I was laughing with him was because he tried to get me to say that you and I had something to do with your pops being murdered. I told him he got his facts wrong.*

So, you didn't say anything about me? I wrote after he handed me the ink pen again.

He wrote, *Fuck no! You're like my family! I would die first before I snitch on you or Dylan.*

Instead of taking the ink pen out of Nick's hand, I embraced him. It felt good to see that Nick hadn't crossed to the other side. Now I didn't feel alone anymore. I leaned over and whispered into his ear, "Come on, let's get out of here."

Nick followed me out of the kitchen. I grabbed my car keys and handbag from the coffee table and then we both exited my apartment.

Chapter 25

Gotta Be Careful

Nick convinced me to get in the car with him when we entered the parking garage. "Those lame-ass cops probably bugged your car, so let's take mine," he said.

"All right," I replied and followed him to his Range Rover SUV.

After I climbed inside of the truck, I buckled my seat belt and locked my door. I can't say why I locked my door; I just did it. I think that maybe I did it because I thought it was a coping mechanism to make me feel safe. If that is the case, then I fully embrace it.

Once we were out of the parking garage and on the road heading to his apartment across town, Nick felt comfortable to talk. He started the conversation by saying, "A traffic cop pulled me over and threatened to arrest me if I didn't follow him down to the police precinct. So I did, and when I got down there, he pulled me into that interrogation room you saw me in. Then that detective walked in and started asking me all kinds of questions to see if I had something to do with your pops getting murdered. I started laughing and asked him where he got his information from because they took him for a ride."

"Well, when he came in the room to talk to me, he had me

believing that you told him that I had something to do with my father's murder."

"I hope you didn't feed into that bullshit!"

"Don't you think that if I did, they'd still have me locked up right now?"

"True," Nick agreed. "So how did they get you?" he wanted to know.

"Detective Grimes must've put out an APB on my car because a uniformed officer stopped me and when he found out who I was, he went back to his car and called that piece of shit. And less than five minutes later, Detective Grimes showed up and hauled me down to the precinct."

"So, how did you get out?"

"I hired an attorney this morning. So, after I arrived at the police station, I called him and he came."

"You know they got the surveillance tape from the IHOP spot we parked my truck in."

Surprised by this information, my heart rate immediately picked up. "How do you know that?" I asked.

"Because the detective told me."

"Are you serious right now?" I asked him. I couldn't believe my ears. Did Detective Grimes have some strong evidence against me? If he did, then why did he let me go?

"Yes, I am," he answered me.

"Well, what are we going to do?" I wanted to know.

"We're gonna go back to my apartment and come up with a plan. We've gotta stay a couple of steps ahead of those fucking cops or they're gonna lock us up and then give our asses a life sentence."

"I'll die first before I let those motherfuckers lock me up."

"Don't talk like that. Just let me do the thinking and the talking and we're gonna be fine. Okay?"

"Okay," I replied, though I wasn't sold on his idea.

From the moment I walked into Nick's apartment, a huge weight was lifted from my shoulders. I threw my handbag onto the sectional in Nick's living room and then I flopped down next to it. "Want something to drink? Juice? Bottled water?" Nick asked me as he headed into the kitchen.

"Yeah, a bottle of water will be fine," I told him.

While Nick was getting me a bottle of water from the refrigerator, I grabbed the TV remote and powered on the television. I sifted through the channels until I came across a local news station. A couple of seconds later, Nick came out of the kitchen with the bottle of water in hand. After he handed it to me, he sat down about two feet away from me. "We've gotta figure out a way to stay off the radar," he started off.

There was an infomercial playing so I turned my attention towards Nick. "How do you expect for us to do that?" I asked him.

"First of all, we need to change phone services. Get rid of these phones we have and get new ones. And after we do that, we're gonna have to talk as little as possible while we're on them."

"Do you think Detective Grimes is going to come after us again?"

"Of course, I do. So, we gotta be ready when he does."

"I swear, when I saw you talking to him in that room there was no question in my mind that he had you feeding information about me."

Nick smiled. "Kira, I've already told you that you and Dylan are like family to me. There is no cop on earth that would ever get me to talk about you. I would die first before I turn into a snitch."

"Nick, I already know this, which is why I was taken aback when I saw you talking to Detective Grimes."

Nick chuckled. "I probably would've thought the same thing if I saw you sitting in there."

"It's all good. I'm just glad that we got all this ironed out now."

"Me too," he agreed, and then he changed the subject. "What's gonna happen with your pops? Are you going to take care of his funeral arrangements or what?"

"Yeah, I have to. It's not like I have any brothers or sisters."

"Where do they have his body?"

"Right now, it's down at the coroner's office."

"Have you been down there yet?"

I took a deep breath and then I exhaled. "Yes, I went down there after I left the police station."

"Did you see his body?"

I hung my head low to prevent Nick from seeing the tears forming around my eyes. Nick saw this and scooted closer to me. "I know you're hurt," he said as he lifted my head back up and turned my face around so that he and I could have direct eye contact. By this time, I was sobbing nonstop. Nick used the back of his hands to wipe the tears away from my cheeks. Then he wrapped his arms around my shoulders. "Nick, when the autopsy examiner started pulling the white sheet away from his head, all I saw was his burnt skull, so I told him to stop. And then I walked out of there," I explained while continuing to sob.

Nick pulled me closer into his arms. "Don't worry. It's gonna be all right." He tried to console me.

"No, it's not. Nick, who kills their own father?" I questioned him while trying to make sense of my actions.

"Look, I know you feel bad about it now. But time will heal your wounds."

"But I can't get that image out of my head. His head looked like a ball of ashes. So just imagine how the rest of his body looked." I cried. My father's murder will probably haunt me for the rest of my life.

"Listen, Kira, you got to stop blaming yourself."

"Then who else can I blame? I'm the one that lured him out of his house and told him to get in the truck. And I'm the one that pulled the trigger and set the truck on fire," I snapped, and then I stood up on my feet. "I think Detective Grimes is going to find out that I killed my father," I continued. By this time, I had become extremely paranoid. A couple of seconds later, I started pacing back and forth in Nick's living room.

Nick stood up and rushed towards me. "Kira, you're gonna have to be quiet before someone hears you. My neighbors are pretty nosy too," he warned me after he grabbed me into his arms again.

While Nick tried to console me, my cell phone started ringing. I was afraid to grab my phone from my handbag, so Nick did it for me. "It's Dylan," he said after he picked up the phone. He answered it on the third ring. "Hello," he said and then he pressed down on the speakerphone button and that's when we both heard the recorded message.

"You have a pre-paid call from Dylan, an inmate at the Miami-Dade County jail, to accept this call press one now." Nick pressed the one button on my phone and waited for Dylan to say hello. Two seconds later, Dylan did just that.

"Hello," he said.

Nick pulled me closer to him while he held my cell phone in his hand. "Hey, baby, what's up?" I replied, trying to prevent him from hearing me cry. But it didn't work. Dylan knew me like the back of his hand. He knew something was wrong with me. "Are you crying?" he asked me.

"No, I had something stuck in my throat," I lied.

"Okay, well, I'm calling you because my lawyer just came to see me and told me that your pops was murdered. What happened?"

"I don't know. All I know is that he was burned up in an SUV."

"Damn! That's fucked up!"

"Yeah, I know."

"So, my attorney told me that you stopped by his office today too."

"Yeah, he called me and told me to stop by there. He was the one to break the news to me about my father," I replied, my voice still cracking.

"Baby, are you crying?" he questioned me once again. His voice sounded so sympathetic.

"Yeah, Dylan, she's standing here crying. I'm trying to get her to cheer up," Nick interjected. I was so glad that Nick answered Dylan's question for me. The way I was feeling right now, I probably would've told Dylan that I killed my father.

"Well, I got some good news," Dylan blurted out.

"What's up?" Nick asked him.

"My lawyer also told me that he was going down to the court clerk's office to file a petition for the case to be thrown out."

"That's good, baby. I'm happy for you," I managed to say, while I sobbed more than ever.

"Yeah, man, that's good to know. Can't wait to see you back out here on these streets," Nick expressed.

"Yeah, me too."

"So, did your lawyer tell you how long it's gonna take for the motion to go through?" Nick asked.

"Yeah, he said it shouldn't take more than a week. In most cases, he said that he's seen motions go through in one or two days. So, that's what I'm hoping will happen in my case."

"I hope so too because you shouldn't be in there in the first place. Those fucking judges down there are just as corrupt as the cops," Nick stated.

"Yeah, they did me wrong. But I'll be all right," Dylan acknowledged. "So, have the cops been by our house to talk to Kira?" Dylan continued.

"Detective Grimes has been harassing me daily since he locked you up," I interjected. "And I just found out that he's handling my father's murder case too. He had one of the traffic cops pull me over earlier today and then he had them take me down to the police station so he could interrogate me."

"So, what did he say?"

"He couldn't say much because I hired an attorney named Mr. Kessler. And when Mr. Kessler found out I was down there, he came and picked me up."

"Well, baby, I'm sorry to hear about your father because I know you loved him very much. But look on the bright side. I should be getting out in the next few days. And once that happens, I promise I will never leave your side again. Okay?"

"Okay," I replied, my voice barely audible.

"Good. Now let me speak to Nick," Dylan instructed.

"I'm right here. Kira got you on speaker."

"Nick, take care of her."

"Don't worry. I'll look after her," Nick assured him.

"Other than that, is everything else cool?"

"Yeah, man, everything is good."

"What's up with my mother and sister? Ask Kira did she get a chance to talk to them yet?"

"Tell him no," I uttered softly.

"She said no, man. She hasn't spoken to them."

"I wonder what's going on with them."

"Me and Kira went by there sometime last week because Bruce wouldn't let Kira talk to your moms."

"Whatcha mean, Bruce wouldn't let Kira talk to my mother?" Dylan asked suspiciously. I could also hear the anger reeling up inside of him.

"When Kira went by your mom's house to check on her, Bruce answered the door and told Kira that your mother was asleep and that she's not allowed to come inside the house. So, then Kira told Bruce that she had to use the bathroom and that she promised not to wake your moms up if he let her into the house."

"Did he let her in?"

"Nope. He got smart with her and told her to get off their property."

"Come on, Nick, please don't tell me that that coward disrespected Kira like that," Dylan begged.

"I wish I could, but that's not what happened."

"Yo, Nick, I swear I'm gonna hurt that old-ass man when I get out of here. I'm so fucking tired of his whack ass trying to throw his weight around that house like he bought it. My father put my mother in that damn house. Not him!" Dylan roared.

"Dylan, don't get all worked up, man. Just concentrate on getting out of there and Kira and I will handle the rest," Nick said, intending to ease Dylan's mind.

"Do me a favor," Dylan said.

"Sure, what's up?"

"Go by my mom's spot again. And if Bruce still won't let y'all see my mama, then call my sister because she got a key to the house. She'll let y'all in the house," Dylan instructed.

"A'ight, I gotcha. I'll get it done today," Nick assured him.

"Baby, are you still there?" Dylan yelled through the phone. I knew he was referring to me when he said *baby*.

"Yes, I'm still here," I responded. By this time, I wasn't crying as much as I was when he first called.

"Well, keep your head up, baby, and this will all be over real soon. Okay?"

"Okay," I replied loud enough for him to hear me.

"I love you."

"I love you too," I told him.

Dylan and Nick talked for another twenty seconds before the phone call was disconnected by the fifteen-minute time limit. After Nick handed me my cell phone, I walked back over to the sectional, stuffed the phone back into my purse, and then I lay down next to it. "Do you want a blanket?" he asked me.

"No, I'm fine. I just wanna lie here for a moment so I can think about my next move," I told him.

"Well, if you need anything, I'll be in my bedroom," he replied, and then he left the room.

Immediately after Nick walked out of the living room, I snuggled up in a fetal position in the right-side corner of the sectional and then I closed my eyes. Nick's entire apartment was quiet. It was so quiet that you could hear a pin drop. But as fate would have it, that small ounce of solitude went straight down the drain when I heard Nick arguing with someone on his cell phone. "What the fuck do you want now?" he roared. He sounded like he was at his wit's end.

"Bianca, I've got a lot of shit going on, so I refuse to deal with your bullshit right now," I heard Nick say. I couldn't hear anything Bianca was saying, but whatever it was, it sent Nick over the edge. He started screaming at the top of his voice. "Are you fucking deaf? Didn't I just say that I wasn't dealing with your shit?" Then he fell silent.

Less than three seconds later he said, "I'll tell you what, lose my number, you stupid bitch!" I didn't hear anything else from that point, so I figured that he hung up on her. What a way to end a conversation!

Chapter 26

A Family Affair

My mission in life is to make money, get married, have kids, and grow old with the man I love. I've only accomplished one thing on that list, and that was getting the money. So, I wonder, why haven't I been able to do any of those other things? Well, the answer is easy. With all of the drama I've come across in my lifetime, having kids would not have been a smart thing to do. Who knows, maybe one day it will happen. And then again, maybe it won't.

—◆—

I wasn't aware that I had dozed off for a couple of hours until Nick woke me up. "Come on, we gotta go and check on Mrs. Daisy," Nick said as he tapped me on my shoulders.

"What time is it?" I asked, trying to get my eyes focused from the sudden light in the room.

It's a little after five o'clock," he replied.

I rubbed my eyes with the back of my hands and then I stood up on my feet. "Don't you think we should call her first?" I asked.

"Yeah, call her," he agreed.

I grabbed my cell phone from my handbag and then I dialed

Mrs. Daisy's phone number. It had been a couple of days since I'd tried to contact her, so there was no doubt in my mind that I'd be able to talk to her today. Unfortunately for me, that didn't happen because her voicemail picked up on the first ring. I looked at Nick and said, "It went straight to voicemail."

"Call it again," he instructed me.

I cleared the line and dialed Mrs. Daisy's cell phone number again. And like the first time, it went straight to voicemail. "It went to voicemail again," I told him.

"Call Sonya and see if she'll answer her phone," Nick suggested.

Once again I cleared the line and then I called Sonya's cell phone number. Surprisingly, Sonya's cell phone started ringing. It rang five times and then her voicemail picked up. "Her voicemail came on so I'm gonna leave a message," I said.

"Hey, Sonya, this is Kira. I've been trying to get in contact with you in the last couple of days. So when you get this message, call me back," I said, and then I disconnected the call.

"Something is going on with these two because I've called them a few times in the last couple of days and they haven't returned any of my calls."

"Get your things and let's go over there," Nick said and then he headed towards the front door. After I slipped on my shoes and grabbed my purse, I followed in his footsteps.

On our way across town, Nick and I didn't talk much, for fear that the homicide detectives may have bugged his truck. We did, however, chat a little bit about his new girlfriend Bianca. "So, have you calmed down from the conversation you had earlier with Bianca?"

"Yeah, I've calmed down a little," he replied, without taking his eyes off the road.

"So how long have you been dating her?" I wanted to know.

"Not long, a month maybe."

"Sounds like the honeymoon stages are already over."

"They were over after I fucked her the second time."

"What happened?" I continued to question him. I needed something to take my mind off my father's death.

"She's starting to get a little too clingy. After I slept with her for the second time, she figured she could question me about my every move. I don't do well when women try to control me."

"You should've told her that before you fucked her the first time."

"Maybe I should've. Think it's too late to do it now?" he asked me and cracked a smile.

I smiled back at him. "Yeah, pretty much."

———※———

The sun began to set as we pulled into Mrs. Daisy's neighborhood. For some reason, anxiety crept into my body. I tried to figure out why I was feeling this way, but my mind wouldn't let me go there. Then it came to me that we might run into Bruce again and have to deal with his shenanigans. I hoped it didn't happen because we already had enough shit going on.

When Nick pulled up curbside in front of Mrs. Daisy's house, none of the cars were there. The driveway was completely empty. "I wonder where everyone is?" Nick spoke up.

"I know sometimes Bruce works at night. So, maybe Mrs. Daisy is at Sonya's apartment."

"Well, I guess that's where we're headed," Nick told me as he drove away from the curb. "Try calling her again. Who knows, she may answer it this time."

I grabbed my cell phone from my purse and dialed Sonya's cell phone number again. I put the call on speaker so Nick could hear the conversation if Sonya answered the call this time. The phone rang six times and then the call went to voicemail. *You reached the right person, but at the wrong time. Leave me a message at the sound of the beep.* BEEP!

"Hey, Sonya, this is Kira again. I just left your mother's house but no one was home. So, now Nick and I are headed over to your place. Call me back," I said and then I ended the call.

"Do you think Sonya's home?" Nick asked with uncertainty.

"I don't know, but we'll find out," I replied, and then I turned my focus to the buildings and cars we passed on our way to Sonya's house. I started thinking about the choices I've made in my life and how I've escaped death on three occasions. And during that time, I lost my husband, Ricky, my cousin Nikki, and my grandmother. I can say that God has protected me all of these years. Without Him, I can't say where I'd be. I can't even say how I'd repay Him.

Sonya lived in a townhouse only ten minutes away from Mrs. Daisy. Her neighborhood was in a middle-class area called Coral Gables. She shared the townhouse with her husband, Glenn, who was away in Afghanistan. He and Sonya didn't have kids together, but he did have two from a previous relationship. Sonya has been very vocal about not being able to have kids with Glenn. But she vowed to give him one before she left this earth. Sonya had the attitude of a fighter, so I knew she would never give up.

As Nick pulled his truck into the parking lot where Sonya's townhouse was located, we noticed that the kitchen lights were on but her car wasn't anywhere in sight. "I don't think she's here," I stated.

"Why you say that?"

"Because her car isn't here."

"Her car could be anywhere, so I'm gonna knock on the door," Nick insisted.

I watched Nick as he got out of his truck and walked up to

the front door of Sonya's townhouse. He stood there and knocked on the door a few times and then he walked over to the kitchen window that was situated near the porch. He peered through the window for what seemed like three seconds and then he turned around and walked back off the porch. Two teenage girls were standing near a tree next to Sonya's townhouse with their eyes glued to their cell phones, so Nick stopped and started speaking to them.

A minute or two later he returned to the truck and had a mouthful to say. "Those little girls are friends, and one of them lives in the third house down while the other one lives in the row of town houses across the street. So, I asked them if they knew Sonya and they said they did. And then when I asked them when was the last time they saw her, they said they hadn't seen her in a couple of days."

"Maybe she's at work. She's been known to work double shifts at the nursing home," I stated.

"You think we should go up to her job?" Nick asked.

I mulled over his question for a second and then I said, "No, we don't have to do all of that. But I do think we should leave her a note on her door. This way she'll know that we stopped by."

"Okay, well write her a note and I'll stick it in the crack of the front door."

"I'm on it," I told him while I searched my purse for a pen and a piece of scrap paper. After sifting through my things, I found an ink pen and an old utility bill envelope. I flipped it over and proceeded to write the note. *Hey Sonya, where have you been? Nick and I have been looking for you. So, call us! Kira.*

Immediately after I wrote the note, I handed it to Nick and watched him as he stepped out of the truck and walked back onto Sonya's porch. He opened up the screen door and slid the note into the crack near the lock. Once he secured the note he turned around and walked back off the porch.

"You think the note is gonna stay in that same spot until she comes home?"

"It should. I pushed it in that crack as far as I could."

"Okay, so if you did it, then it should be good."

"Well, let's get out of here," Nick said as he drove away from Sonya's town house.

Chapter 27

What Now?

For the last couple of days, I'd been staying at Nick's apartment. Nick insisted that I do this, at least until Dylan was released from jail. I obliged because I didn't want to be at home alone. The gruesome images of me shooting my father would not go away. I thought about it day and night. To make matters worse, I'd been getting one phone call after the next from the city coroner's office, telling me I needed to have my father's body picked up in the next few days or they would be forced to cremate him. So, I got up the gumption and called Dexter's Funeral Home and gave them the green light to pick his body up and start funeral arrangements and I will pay for everything.

Not too much longer after I hung up with the director, I got a call from my attorney, Mr. Kessler. I was sitting at the kitchen table with Nick, eating pancakes and sausages that he picked up from the IHOP restaurant. I put the call on speaker so I could eat and talk at the same time. "Hello, Mr. Kessler."

"Hi, Kira, how are you?" he replied.

"Not too good. Just got off the phone with the funeral director from Dexter's Funeral Home, so I'm not in the best of spirits."

"When is the funeral?"

"In four days."

"Are you the only child?"

"Yes, I'm the only child."

"What about other family members? Do they live in the area?"

"No. I'm the only family member left on my dad's side. I do have a few cousins on my mother's side. But I'm not close with them at all. The last time I heard, they were living in Virginia."

"Oh, wow! But, okay," Mr. Kessler said nonchalantly and then he changed the subject. "Well, I called you because I got a call from Detective Grimes. He wants you and me to come down to the police station later so he can ask you more questions concerning your father's murder. So, will you be available in a couple of hours?"

"Do I have a choice?"

"Well, you do, but I think it would be wise to go down there and answer whatever questions he may have for you so you can finally get it behind you."

"Can we set it up for tomorrow?" I wanted to know. I needed to know if I had any options.

"I have a trial coming up, so I'm gonna be busy for the rest of the week."

"Well, can we do it next week?" I asked. I knew I was pressing my luck.

"I don't think Detective Grimes wants to wait that long."

"I don't care what he wants," I barked. I was getting irritated just thinking about how much of a bully Detective Grimes was. I had the right to make decisions concerning my well-being. So, if I didn't want to see that whack-ass cop today then I should have that option.

"I understand where you're coming from. But as your attorney, I have to advise you that if you decide not to go to do the interview with the detective today, just know that this is an ongoing investigation, so if they find something that links you to the murder, they will come and arrest you."

"I don't care what kind of evidence they find. I loved my father and I would never do anything to hurt him."

"I believe you. But I'm not the one who needs convincing."

"To hell with Detective Grimes. Tell him to leave me alone and go and find the real killer," I spat. Mr. Kessler realized that this conversation was making me upset so he found a nice way to end the call on a good note.

"Well, I'm gonna call Detective Grimes back and let him know that you're not available today because you're mourning your father. So let's see if that works."

"Perfect. And I'll wait to hear back from you."

"Sounds great. Talk to you later," he said, and then I disconnected our call.

"So, that cop is trying to get you to go back down there, huh?" Nick asked between chews.

"Yeah, and you heard what I said," I replied.

"You know he's only trying to scare you into confessing."

"Yes, I know. But I'm not falling for his tactics."

"Yeah, fuck him!" Nick agreed as he continued to dig into his pancakes and sausages.

I, on the other hand, couldn't enjoy the meal like I had before Mr. Kessler called. The mere mention of Detective Grimes spoiled my appetite. I pushed my plate of food away from me and went into deep thought.

"What's on your mind?" Nick wanted to know.

"I'm just thinking about everything that's going on. I need to go home so I can get my thoughts together," I said and stood up from the table.

"You're leaving now?"

"Yeah, I gotta get out of here."

"Are you coming back?"

"Yes, I'll back later," I assured him and then I left.

En route to my apartment, my cell phone started ringing. I hit the Bluetooth function on the dashboard of my car and the phone number of the caller appeared. It was Mrs. Daisy, so I immediately pressed the answer button and said hello but I didn't get a response. So I said hello again and she didn't respond. "Mrs. Daisy, are you there? Can you hear me?" I yelled. And once again I didn't get a reply, so I disconnected the call. I started to call her cell phone back, but I figured her reception wasn't working once again and when she got a chance she would call me back. I did, however, send her a text message that read, Mrs. Daisy, your son & I are worried about you. I stopped by your house last night. I even went by Sonya's house. Give me a call please and that way we will know that you're all right.

Immediately after I sent off the text message my cell phone started ringing again. I looked at the dashboard of my car and saw that the call was coming from Mr. Kessler, so I pressed the speakerphone function and answered his call. "Hi, Kira," he spoke.

"Hi, Mr. Kessler," I spoke back.

"Okay, so I just spoke with Detective Grimes and he wants to interview you today. He also said that if we don't come in today, he's going to have you indicted on murder charges."

"Can he do that?"

"Well, so far it seems like he has a lot of circumstantial evidence against you. And with that circumstantial evidence, he would be able to get you indicted. Now, that evidence may not hold up in court. But you don't want to go through the process of going to court to beat those charges. I think that if we go down there and talk to him, we could get you cleared as a potential suspect. And then we won't have to worry about him again," Mr. Kessler explained.

Within minutes, my head started spinning and the contents in my stomach started rumbling. The mere thought of going back down to the police station and allowing Detective Grimes to interview me concerning my father's murder was not sitting well with me. I mean, what if he wanted me to take a polygraph test? And what if he started questioning my whereabouts during the time my father was murdered, and I couldn't provide him with a solid alibi? I knew this guy would try to back me up in a corner, gut me like a fish, and then eat me for dinner. Hopefully, Mr. Kessler wouldn't allow Detective Grimes to do those things to me.

So after mulling over the conversation that Mr. Kessler had with Detective Grimes, I finally agreed to sit down and talk to him. "What time are we supposed to be there?"

"Would you be able to meet me within the hour?" Mr. Kessler asked me.

"I'm in the middle of something right now. But I could meet you in two hours," I told him.

"Okay, sounds great. So, meet me in front of the station at one thirty."

"Will do," I said, and then we both ended the call.

I started to call Nick back and let him know that Mr. Kessler convinced me to talk to Detective Grimes today just in case something comes up and he needed to know where I was. But at the last minute, I decided not to. I thought about the possibility that the cops might have my cell phone wired, so I figured the less the cops heard me talking to Nick over the phone the better off he and I would be.

◦◦◦

In a matter of an hour and a half, I went home, relaxed a little, and changed clothes before heading back out to meet

Mr. Kessler at the police station. On my way out of my apartment, my cell phone beeped, notifying me that someone had just texted me, so I grabbed it from the inside pocket of my purse and opened the notification. The text message came from Sonya. Kira, I've been working long shifts this past week, but don't worry I'm fine. I will call you as soon as I get a break.

I texted back. Ok, cool. Handle your business.

Right when I was putting my cell phone away, it started ringing. I looked at the caller ID and saw that it was Mr. Kessler calling me. I answered the call immediately. "Hello," I said.

"Hey, are you on your way?"

"Yes, I am. I should be there in the next fifteen minutes."

"Okay, great. See you then," Mr. Kessler said and then we ended our call.

Chapter 28

People vs. Kira Wade

Mr. Kessler was waiting outside the police precinct like he said he would, so I parked my car, got out of it, and scurried over to him.

"Are you ready?" he asked me.

"As ready as I'll ever be."

"Well, this is how we're gonna handle things. If he asks you a question that I feel will incriminate you, I will interject and recite a legal code that prohibits him from manipulating you into answering it. Or if the question makes you feel uncomfortable, then just tell him that you plead the Fifth."

"Wow! That's it?"

"Pretty much."

I took a deep breath and then I exhaled. "Well, I guess I'm ready,"

I announced.

"Well then, let's go," Mr. Kessler said.

I followed Mr. Kessler into the building and then I followed him down a very long hallway. "We're going to make a left turn at this next corner," he instructed me and then he said, "We are also going to be in the room with two detectives. They may try to intimidate you, but remember, I'm there so take your time when you answer their questions, and again, if you're un-comfortable with it then I want you to let me know."

I let out a long sigh. "Will do," I replied, feeling nervous.

After Mr. Keesler gave me a pep talk, we entered the same interview room that Nick was in a couple of days prior. I instantly got chills running down my spine. "After you," Mr. Kessler said as he stepped aside so I could walk into the room ahead of him.

"Good afternoon!" said Detective Grimes. He was sitting in the interview room alone.

"Yes, good afternoon," replied Mr. Kessler.

I gave him a look of death and then I quickly turned my head in the opposite direction. Quite frankly, it wasn't a good afternoon in my eyes. It was kind of screwed up.

"Are you interviewing Ms. Wade alone?" Mr. Kessler wanted to know as he took a seat at the conference table. I sat down next to him.

"No, Detective Brady will be in here in a second," Detective Grimes stated. "Oh wait, there he is," Detective Grimes continued after he saw his partner walk through the door.

"I take it you guys were just talking about me," Detective Brady said.

"As a matter of fact, we were," Mr. Kessler acknowledged, giving him a half smile.

I watched Detective Brady as he closed the door to the room and sat in the chair next to Detective Grimes. I looked at him from head to toe and quickly realized that he was one of the detectives roaming around at my apartment the day my father was shot. He looked at me briefly and then he turned his focus towards Detective Grimes.

"Okay, Mr. Kessler, are you and your client ready to began?" Detective Grimes asked after he opened up a manila folder placed on the table in front of him.

Mr. Kessler looked at me and asked me if I was ready and I

gave him a head nod, even though I felt otherwise. Detective Grimes cleared his throat and started by asking me where I was on the night my father was murdered. I looked at him and then I turned my attention towards Mr. Kessler. Was Detective Grimes serious right now? Did he really want me to answer that question so soon? I mean, the interview just started. He was seriously going for the jugular with this interview. "Are you going to answer the question?" Detective Grimes asked me.

"What night was that?" I asked, trying to delay answering the question.

"It was the night of the twentieth," Detective Grimes replied.

"And what day was that?" I asked, continuing to delay answering the question.

"Ms. Wade, it was Saturday night. Just four days ago," Detective Grimes explained.

"That was so long ago. I don't remember," I finally answered.

"Ms. Wade, we just had you here in the station two days ago," Detective Grimes pointed out.

"Are you sure it was two days ago? It feels like it was longer than that," I said nonchalantly.

"Come on, Ms. Wade, stop bullshitting and wasting our time. We know you killed your father," Detective Brady interjected.

"I'm afraid you're wrong. I wouldn't harm a strand of hair on my father's head," I said matter-of-factly. I gave them the appearance that I wasn't nervous or intimidated by them.

"Well, why won't you answer the question?" Detective Brady barked.

"Which one was that?" I asked, trying to play dumb.

"We only asked you one question, Ms. Wade. Now tell us your whereabouts the night your father was murdered." De-

WIFEY'S NEXT DEADLY HUSTLE / 157

tective Grimes huffed. I could tell that he was getting extremely irritated with me.

"I don't remember," I answered.

"Well, guess what, Ms. Wade? We know where you were," Detective Grimes blurted out as he leaned on the table that separated us.

"So, if you know, then why am I here?" I replied sarcastically. Because right now I'm getting a little hot underneath my collar.

"You're here because we want to give you a chance to tell us the whole story before we draw our own conclusions. And if we have to draw our own conclusions, then you're going to be up shit creek when we're done charging and convicting you of murder," Detective Grimes stated.

"Well, I'm sorry because I don't have a story to tell you," I told him.

"Hold that thought for a moment," Detective Grimes said, and then he stood up from his seat. He walked over to the door of the interview room and opened it. "Hey, Mitchell, can you come in here for a minute?" he yelled out.

I had no idea who Detective Grimes was calling, but the thought of someone walking around the corner got me a little nervous. I heard footsteps walking towards the door and when the person appeared before everyone in the room, I instantly became sick on my stomach. "Ms. Wade, do you know this man?" Detective Grimes asked me after the man entered the interview room.

"No, I'm afraid not," I lied. But I knew the white man standing before me was one of the traffic officers that pulled Nick and me over in front of the IHOP restaurant. I also knew that I was knee-deep in shit if these officers put two and two together.

"Well, that's mighty funny because Officer Mitchell here

says that he pulled you and your buddy Nick over in the parking lot of the IHOP restaurant the night we pulled your father from that burning SUV. Now does that little bit of information jog your memory some?" Detective Grimes asked sarcastically.

I looked at Mr. Kessler, who by now was looking at me. I wanted him to give me direction as to how to handle this question, but he seemed a bit clueless himself. So, I turned my focus back towards Detective Grimes and Officer Mitchell. "I don't know what y'all want me to say," I finally said, even though what I just said didn't make a bit of sense.

"Tell us why you and Nick were less than a half mile away from where your father was murdered!" Detective Grimes roared. He was irritated with me now.

"Haven't you heard of a coincidence? Because that's what that was," I finally said.

Detective Grimes pressed the issue. "Tell us why you were in the parking lot of the IHOP."

"Because we were hungry."

"So what did you eat?" Detective Grimes wanted to know.

"We never went into the restaurant."

"Why not?" Detective Grimes continued his questions.

"Because we got into an argument and I lost my appetite."

"Who got into an argument?" Detective Grimes probed more.

"Nick and I."

"Why were you two arguing?"

"I don't remember," I lied. Nick and I made up a story to throw Officer Mitchell and his partner off, to prevent them from associating us with my father's murder.

"Well, do you remember luring your father from his home on the night that he was murdered?"

"Of course, I don't."

"Why not?"

"Because it didn't happen."

"Ms. Wade, do I look naïve to you?" Detective Grimes asked me.

"I'm sorry, but I don't know what naïve looks like," I responded sarcastically.

"Well, let me tell you this. You and I both know that your father wouldn't have left his house with someone he didn't know. And I'm certain that he wouldn't have opened his door to a stranger. So, tell us why did you do it?"

"I didn't do anything," I snapped. These cops were trying to railroad me into confessing to my father's murder. Whether they knew it or not, I will take this lie to my grave.

"Well, tell us who did it. Was it Nick?"

"I'm telling you guys right now that you're interrogating the wrong person."

"Well, tell us who we need to interrogate. Give us a name." Detective Grimes continued to press me for answers to his questions.

I let out a long sigh. "I don't know."

"Oh, you know. So, give us the goods."

Frustrated by the constant interrogating, I looked at my attorney and said, "I've had enough of this. Can we leave now?"

"Tell us, why was your father's body in the back seat of that burning SUV?" Detective Grimes blurted out, refusing to let Mr. Kessler respond to my question. "Whoever lured him out of his house, instructed him to get in the back seat. So that means there were two people with him that night. One person was driving and the other person sat next to him in the back-seat. And if you remember, Officer Mitchell can personally ID you and Nick sitting in his truck less than a half mile from where the murder took place."

"Sounds like you've got this whole thing figured out."

"Not quite, but it's coming together."

"Good for you. Can we go now?" I turned around and faced my attorney again.

"Are you guys charging my client with any crimes?" Mr. Kessler asked. His demeanor was that of a very confident man who was ready to go to war for me.

Officer Mitchell and Detective Brady looked at Detective Grimes. "Let me just say that if your client leaves out of here today without assisting me and my partner with this murder investigation, then I won't cut her a deal and I'm gonna push for her to get life in prison without the possibility of parole after I get a grand jury to indict her."

"Why don't you do that, and then we'll see you in court," Mr. Kessler said, and then he stood up from the chair. I stood up next to him. "The only thing you guys have right now is circumstantial evidence and that's not gonna fly in court," Mr. Kessler continued, as he looked every officer in the eye.

After Mr. Kessler dared them to indict me, I looked at all of them and smiled. Several seconds later, Mr. Kessler grabbed his briefcase from the table, and then he looked at me and said, "Let's get out of here."

"I'm sorry you guys couldn't get the information you were looking for. But, I had already told y'all that you were talking to the wrong person," I said as I followed my attorney towards the door.

"Then who should we be talking to, Kira?"

"You guys just don't let up, do you?" I said while I walked by them to get to the door.

"Not when we feel strongly about something."

"Well, don't let me hold you up from finding the real killer."

"I think we already have, considering we just pulled a fresh new set of your fingerprints from the doorknob on the front door of your father's home," Detective Grimes said while I was walking out of the interview room.

I stopped in my tracks after I stepped over the entryway of the door and said, "For your information, I have a key to my father's house, so quite naturally my fingerprints would be there."

"Tell us, when was the last time you were at your father's home?" Detective Brady asked. He had been quiet this whole time until now.

I looked at him and smiled. "I don't remember," I told him and then I walked off with my attorney in tow.

Chapter 29

I'm Watching You

Going back down to the police precinct wasn't something I wanted to do. But I did it anyway. Thankfully, Mr. Kessler shut those cops down because if he hadn't, Detective Grimes and those other two officers would've railroaded me and I would be in a jail cell right now. "I'm so glad that's over," I said as soon as we stepped outside of the building.

"I am too. For a minute there, I thought you were going to say the wrong thing," Mr. Kessler replied.

"I know. I saw your facial expression change a few times when it was time for me to talk," I stated.

"Well, you see how badly they want to charge you with your father's murder. And the fact that they know two people were involved in his murder is a critical key point for this investigation. Speaking of which, why didn't you tell me that you and another gentleman were pulled over less than a half mile from the murder scene?"

"Because I didn't think it was important," I lied. The real reason I didn't tell Mr. Kessler we were pulled over by that officer was because I had no idea that Detective Grimes was going to find out, since there was no traffic ticket issued.

He pressed me. "Are you being straightforward with me? Now, remember I'm on your side."

"Yes, I am." I tried to assure him. But I don't think he believed me.

"Well, tell me, exactly when was the last time you were at your father's house?" His questions continued.

"I'm not sure. But it wasn't too long after he got out of the hospital," I replied, trying to give him the most sincere expression I could muster up.

"I'll tell you what, try to find out exactly when you were at your father's house because it's important that we establish a timeline so that those detectives can rule you out as a suspect."

"Okay. I can do that."

"All right, now be careful. Don't talk to anyone while this investigation is going on. Do I make myself clear?"

"Absolutely."

"And don't forget to call me if you need anything."

"I will," I replied as we shook hands and then we parted ways.

It felt like a weight was lifted from my shoulders after the interrogation was over. Detective Grimes certainly tried to railroad me when he brought that traffic cop into the interrogation room. I know one thing: If that traffic cop would've tested my hands for gunpowder I would be standing in front of a magistrate trying to get a bond. If you are convicted of murder in the state of Florida, the justice system will try to throw the book at you. And if the murder victim is a well-respected judge like my father was, his peers in the court system will try to give you the death penalty. I can't have that. No way.

After I sat down in the driver's seat of my car, I watched Mr. Kessler as he drove away. To see him driving a late-model

$150,000 Porsche sent a clear message that he was living a good life. I couldn't tell you how peaceful his life was, but if he was charging all of his clients the amount of money he was charging me, he was a very rich man, and rich men buy peace and happiness all of the time. It's the way of the world.

When I started up the ignition, I realized that I needed to fill up my car. My gas tank was almost empty, so I drove to the nearest gas station, which was only three blocks away from the police station. I took my debit card out of my purse and stepped out of the car. Immediately after I stepped up to the gas pump, I swiped my card, and once I was authorized to pump the gas I took the hose and started filling my tank up with the gas.

While I was pumping the gas into my car, I couldn't help but wonder if Detective Grimes was telling the truth when he mentioned that the forensic investigators had pulled fresh fingerprints that belong to me from my father's doorknob. I mean, how fresh could they have been? And was there a thing call fresh fingerprints? Like I said, I have a key to my father's house, so whether the fingerprints were new or not, they have no evidence that would implicate me as being the murderer. Now I was caught off guard when Detective Grimes stated that they knew that there had to be at least two killers because my father was sitting in the back seat of the truck. I almost had a heart attack when he mentioned it. But once again my attorney was present and he saved me every time he felt he needed to. I guess I can say that was money well spent.

The gas meter stopped at thirty-five dollars, and while I was putting the hose back into the gas pump, a car pulled up behind me. I looked over my shoulder and saw two men sitting in the front seat. I recognized both men. But I only knew the name of the man sitting in the passenger seat. I forced a smile on my face as I waved at him. "Hey, Kendrick, what's up?" I asked while I walked slowly towards the car.

Kendrick slightly leaned his head out of the passenger-side window. "Chilling!" he replied as he watched me approach him.

Anxiety crept inside my stomach like it always does when I'm around someone or something that could cause my demise. So, I forced myself to put one foot in front of the other and before I knew it, I was standing alongside the passenger-side door.

"So, what did they want this time?" he continued.

"Who?" I wondered aloud.

"Don't play dumb with me," Kendrick hissed. He instantly became irritated with me. "I'm talking about the fucking cops. I saw you and your lawyer walk inside the precinct not too long ago."

"If you think your name came up, then you're wrong," I told him.

"What did y'all talk about?" Kendrick wanted to know.

I was taken aback by his question so I hesitated for a moment. The first thought that came to my mind was that I'd be a damn fool if I told him the real reason why I was talking to the homicide detectives. But then again, I knew I couldn't lie to him. Kendrick has always been able to detect when someone was lying to him, so I was at a crossroads.

"Are you gonna stand there and look stupid, or are you going to tell me what you and the cops were talking about?"

"They were asking me questions about my father's murder," I forced myself to say.

"What kind of questions?"

"They wanted to know when was the last time I talked to him and seen him."

Kendrick chuckled. "So, they looking at you as a suspect, huh?"

"It's just a formality," I stated nonchalantly.

"But, you and I both know who did it, right?" Kendrick commented.

Once again, taken aback by his question I instantly had chills rolling down my spine. Kendrick was a creepy but dangerous guy. I knew I had to be careful with my words. "I don't understand what you're saying," I replied.

Kendrick sat up in his seat. "Kira, don't play with me. You know that I know you and Nick offed your pops. And I also know that you did it to get your man out of jail. When is he coming home? Today? Tomorrow?"

I stood there dumbfounded and at a loss for words. I honestly didn't know what to say. I felt like I was caught red-handed. "Remember, I know about everything that goes on in the streets of Miami," Kendrick reminded me.

"Whatcha trying to do, set me up?" I uttered from my mouth without even thinking about it first. The words just started rolling off my tongue.

"Come here," Kendrick snapped. He reached his arm out towards me, grabbed ahold of my shirt, and pulled me towards him. Before I knew it, Kendrick had jammed the barrel of a gun into my stomach. "Bitch, get smart with me again and I will put this lead in you so fast, you ain't gonna know what hit you," Kendrick barked.

The impact of Kendrick pushing the gun in my side set off excruciating pains throughout my abdomen. I flinched as my knees started buckling. The only reason I didn't fall was because Kendrick held on to my shirt with a firm grip. "You don't think I would kill you right here, huh?" he continued, giving me a menacing look.

"Yes, I know you would."

"Well, if you know this, then why are you talking shit?" he asked as he pressed the gun farther into my stomach.

"I'm sorry, I just got a lot on my mind right now," I said while tears started falling from my eyes. I was becoming an emotional wreck and I was unsure as to how much more drama my life could take. Kendrick loosened his hold on my shirt when he saw me wiping tears off my face.

"I don't give a damn about your tears, so clean that shit up," he growled. Like a newcomer in boot camp, I stood up straight and wiped my face clear of any tears. "All I came over here to say to you is, I know you whacked your pops, so if I ever find out that you're helping the cops with any information concerning the judge and his wife, you're going down too," he threatened me. "Are we clear?"

I continued to stand there but said absolutely nothing. I did give him a head nod because what could I possibly say? Everything he said was self-explanatory. If I ran my mouth off to the cops, he would make me pay for it.

Without saying another word to me, Kendrick looked at his driver and instructed him to drive away. Less than three seconds later, I was standing there watching Kendrick and his flunky leaving the service station. Boy, did I feel relieved to see him go. And in a flash, I rushed back to my car, hopped inside, and sped out of there as quickly as I could.

Instead of going in the direction of my apartment, I decided to take a long drive out of Miami. Head up to West Palm Beach and turn back around. I knew this trip would give me some R and R. Clearing my mind of all the bullshit I had scrambling in my mind. I had no idea how I was going to release it, but I figured taking this long drive north would help me make sound decisions and get me out of this depressing state of mind. I prayed that it works.

Chapter 30

Wearing a Brave Face

The one-hour drive to never-never land didn't help me like I thought it would. The fact that I murdered my father was going to take more than a drive in south Florida to put my mind at ease. To make matters worse, I had Detective Grimes and Kendrick breathing down my neck. From where I stood, that was a ratio of 2-to-1. Now how in the hell could I compete? I didn't have the mental and physical stamina to go head to head with those guys. I could only take but so much. I knew one thing: If I didn't figure this shit out, I'd probably have a nervous breakdown or worse—commit suicide.

Ten minutes after I turned my car around to head back down south to Miami, my cell phone started ringing. I pulled it out from my purse and homed in on the caller ID. The call was coming from the county jail, so I answered it because I knew it was Dylan calling. After I accepted his call, I waited for him to come on the line. "Hello," he said after the recorded message ended.

"Hi, baby," I replied.

"Where are you?"

"Out taking a drive so I can clear my mind."

"Have you talked to my lawyer?"

"Not since the last time I talked to you. Why you ask?" I wanted to know.

"No reason," he said and paused. The phone line went radio silent. "I've got some good news," he continued.

"What is it?" I asked, even though I suspected that his good news had something to do with him getting out of jail.

"My lawyer stopped by the jail a few minutes ago and told me that I'm going to court in two days, so get ready," he replied cheerfully.

"That's good, baby. I can't wait for you to come home."

"I can't wait either. I'm so fucking happy that this shit is almost over."

"So, will the charges be dismissed or what?"

"Yes, Mr. Berlinsky said he filed a motion to have my charges dismissed." Dylan spoke confidently.

"What time will your case be heard?"

"I believe he said ten o'clock. So, be there at least thirty minutes ahead of time. You know court cases aren't ever called when they're supposed to be."

"Do you think they're going to release you the same day?"

"Of course, they are. They wouldn't have any other reason to keep me."

"So, once they dismiss the charges, they can't come back and charge you again?"

"No, baby, they won't be able to do it."

I let out a long sigh. "Good. Because I don't think I can be out here without you much longer."

"Have you talked to the cops again about your pop's death?" Dylan changed the subject.

"Yes, I spoke to them a few hours ago."

"Did they stop by the house again? Or did they ask you to come down to the precinct?

"They asked me to come down to the precinct."

"So, what did they say?" he asked. It seemed like I was talking to Kendrick all over again. I mean, I just answered that exact same question a little over an hour ago and now I found myself answering it again. But was I going to give Dylan the same answer I gave Kendrick? Nope. I sure wasn't; especially since he was behind bars. Every outgoing call from inmates is closely monitored.

"You know, the usual. Where was I the night my father was murdered? When was the last time I seen him? When was the last time I talked to him, did the conversation end on a good note?"

"I hope those crackers don't think that I hired someone to kill him." Dylan sounded concerned.

"Who cares what they think? I'm so over them and the murders they are investigating."

"I feel the same way, but at the same time, I don't want to get caught up in something that I was never involved in. I see guys coming to this place every day. But I've run into a guy that's in here for a crime that he didn't commit. This jailhouse shit is serious. Locking up guys like me is big business. So, cops are always on the prowl looking for their next victim, which brings me to this: As soon as I get out of here, I want us to go on a trip away from here. Are you down for it?"

"Of course, I am."

"Do you have any suggestions?" he asked me.

"Not really. But I'm sure you'll be able to come up with something."

"Have you had a chance to talk to my mother or sister yet?"

"I haven't spoken with them, but we've been texting back and forth."

"So you haven't gone back over there?"

"Yes, I went by there, but there were no cars in the driveway so I left."

"So, you say you texted my sister too?"

"Yes, I texted her and she finally texted me back and told

me the reason why she hadn't gotten back with me was because she's been working double shifts at her job," I explained.

"What's up with Nick? Is he holding things down out there?"

"Yeah, he's doing his part, so you don't have to worry about him."

"Have the cops left our apartment alone for good?"

"Yes, they have. We don't have to worry about them coming back for anything."

"Okay, all of that sounds good, but tell me, how are you feeling? Tell me what's on your mind."

"Trust me, there aren't enough minutes left on this call for me to tell you what's going on with me."

"Well, when the call cuts off after the fifteen minutes is done, then I'll call you right back," Dylan insisted. I could tell that he wanted me to share my feelings and concerns with him. And believe me, I wanted to tell him that Kendrick jammed a gun into me and threatened to kill me, but right now wasn't the time to do so. What I did do was tell him how much I loved him.

"Baby, I love you and I truly wish that you and I could leave Miami right now and never come back," I expressed, and I meant every word. I thought relocating to Miami from Virginia would be a good thing, but in the end, it turned out to be my worst decision ever. It seems like trouble follows me everywhere I go.

"Just say the word and we will do that."

"You're acting like it's that easy."

"Because it is. You don't work at the car dealership anymore. And what I do I can do anywhere."

"What about our apartment? We just bought it."

"What about it? We can put it on the market and sell it."

"But what about your mother? We just can't leave her here with Bruce."

"We could convince her to come with us."

"Come on, Dylan, you know your mother will not leave Bruce."

"If I tell her to leave 'im, she will."

"Okay, well, let's say that she agrees to leave Bruce; she's not going to leave the house your father bought her. That's just not going to happen. She cherishes that home. There's a lot of memories there."

"You just let me handle her," Dylan said confidently.

"No problem."

Dylan and I talked for another minute and a half. After the call time was up, he called me back. During this call, Dylan wanted to talk about the funeral arrangements planned for my father. When he first brought up the subject, something inside of me wanted to shut the whole conversation down, but when I thought about how the county jail records its inmates' telephone calls, I decided it would be best if I played the part of mourning daughter, rather than an unconcerned bitch.

"So, how is everything coming along with your dad?"

"What do you mean?"

"Are you having a small funeral service? Huge? What?"

"Well, since I don't have any more family in this area, I plan to have a viewing so that the people my dad worked with could stop by and pay their respects. After that, I'm gonna have the funeral home take him where my mother is buried and lay him to rest beside her."

"Who do you have handling the funeral arrangements?"

"Dexter's."

"I've never heard of them. Are they good?"

"I don't know. You're acting like I plan funerals once a month," I replied sarcastically.

"Awww . . . baby, I'm sorry. You know I didn't mean it like that."

"It's okay, I know you didn't mean any harm."

"I'm glad because I love you so much, and the last thing I ever want to do is stress you out. I mean, you already got a lot on your plate."

"Everything will get better, soon enough," I assured him. I only said it so he could stop apologizing. I knew he didn't mean any harm. Dylan was a great guy. And I knew he loved me. And considering what I did to my father, that's a small testament as to how much I loved him.

At the end of our second phone call, he told me to text his sister Sonya and let her know that he'd be home in a day or so. After I assured him that I'd do it, he told me that he loved me and that as soon as he came home he was going to take care of me. Take me away from all of this murder and mayhem, with hopes that we would finally be able to live happily ever after.

Chapter 31

Hold Up! Wait a Minute!

The second after I cleared my phone line from Dylan's call, I texted his sister Sonya and told her the good news. Surprisingly, she texted me right back. Let him know I miss him and I love him very much.

Instead of texting her back, I dialed her cell phone number since I was driving. Her cell phone rang four times before the voicemail picked up. *You reached the right person, but at the wrong time. Leave me a message at the sound of the beep.* BEEP!

"Sonya, this is Kira. I just texted you and you texted me back. What's going on? Hey listen, call me when you get a chance. Dylan is coming home in less than two days, so he wants to see you and your mom. He also wants you to know that he loves you very much. Talk to you soon," I said, and then I ended the voicemail message.

Immediately after I pressed the end button, I cleared the line and dialed Nick's cell phone number. "Hello," he said.

"Hey, Nick, I got some good news," I stated after he answered the phone.

"What's up?"

"I just got off the phone with Dylan. His lawyer got him a new court date and it's two days away."

"Will he be getting out?"

"Yes, that's the plan."

"Well, that's good. How does he feel about it?"

"He sounded pretty happy!"

"What about you? How do you feel knowing that he's getting ready to come home?"

"I can't enjoy the idea of it because I'm trying to cope with my father's death."

"Have you called any of your relatives?" Nick wanted to know.

"My dad had a second cousin, but he died a few years ago of a heart attack."

"What about your grandparents, are they still alive?"

"Nope. My father outlived my mother and his parents. I'm the last one left."

"Are you having a funeral for him?"

"Yes, sort of. Since he had a lot of friends downtown and at the courthouse, I'm gonna allow them to visit his body at the funeral home. And when that's over, I'm gonna have him buried in the cemetery next to my mother."

"So, when is all of this going to take place?"

"In a couple of days."

"So, what's gonna happen to his house?"

"I don't know. I'm gonna eventually have to call his attorney so he can instruct me on what to do."

"I know this is kind of rough for you, but if you need anything just let me know."

"I appreciate that, Nick."

"No problem, baby girl. Just keep your head up."

"I will," I assured him.

Before Nick and I ended our call, I heard a woman in the background making demands on Nick. I knew instantly that it was his new woman, Bianca. "I wish you would hurry up because I didn't come all the way over here to hear you talk on the damn phone," I heard her say.

Chapter 32

This Is Why I Love Him

The courtroom was packed from wall to wall with defendants, their witnesses, their snitches, the cops that arrested them, and the lawyers that were on the payroll. It was becoming a media circus, with the local news station setting up their camera equipment for a trial that was scheduled for eleven this morning. Thank God Dylan's case was going to be called before it.

I took a seat in the third row and waited patiently for Dylan's case to be called. His attorney, Mr. Berlinsky, was front and center, sitting at a table a few feet away from the judge. There were a couple more attorneys huddled around him carrying on a conversation. I wanted to let him know that I was in the courtroom, but no one but attorneys, prosecutors, or courtroom officials were allowed in that area, so I remained seated. I figured he'd see me eventually.

After waiting for thirty minutes, Mr. Berlinsky finally looked in my direction and headed towards me. He was sharp too. I know my fashion labels, and from what I could see, so did he. I looked at him from head to toe and noticed that he had on a two-thousand-dollar custom-made jacket and slacks, thousand-dollar Christian Louboutin drivers, and five-hundred-dollar Gucci cufflinks. This guy was the real deal.

"Got some good news for you," he started off.

I sighed heavily. "Thank God! After everything else that's been going on, I need some good news," I told him.

Mr. Berlinsky smiled as he moved in closer. "Well, I talked to the prosecutor and he agreed to drop charges because of your father's recent death. But, I want you to let Dylan know that even though his charges will be dismissed today, the prosecutors will likely work behind the scenes with hopes of digging up other dirt to make a case against him. So, tell him to be very careful."

"I will. And thank you so much, Mr. Berlinsky," I replied, and then we shook hands.

"No problem. I'm here for you guys anytime," he assured me. But I knew what he meant. As long as we had money, his phone line would always be open. The moment we went broke, he was going to put us on the block list.

After Mr. Berlinsky walked away from me, he headed back up to the front of the courtroom. A few minutes later, Dylan's case was called. I sat there and watched as the courtroom deputy escorted him into the courtroom. I smiled and winked my eye at him as soon as our eyes connected. He smiled back at me and I instantly saw the relief in his facial expression. On this day he finally got his chance of becoming a free man.

"We're here today to address the motion for dismissal on case number 389740-98121," The Caucasian judge announced as he read the case number from the documents placed in front of him.

"Yes, Your Honor, the state's only witness was killed a few days ago, and without this witness, the state will unlikely prevail in this case without their testimony," Mr. Berlinsky stated.

The judge looked at the prosecutor and said, "The plaintiff was the only witness in this case?"

"Yes, Your Honor," the prosecutor replied. I couldn't see

his face, but I could tell by the tone of his voice that he wasn't happy.

The judge looked back down at the file in front of him and then he looked back up. He turned his attention towards Mr. Berlinsky and Dylan, who was standing next to him. "I appreciate the hard work done by the state in investigating this case, and I understand that the motion to dismiss will be frustrating to some," the judge said. "However, when circumstances change after an indictment is issued and our judgment is that a case is no longer likely to be proven beyond a reasonable doubt, it is our duty to the defendant and the court to dismiss that case. And in this case, the witness's statement is inadmissible because it was made before the trial and now is considered hearsay. So, it is my obligation to dismiss this case. The defendant is now free to be released from custody."

I watched him as he signed three documents.

"Thank you, Your Honor," Mr. Berlinsky said.

"Yes, thank you, Your Honor," I heard Dylan say afterwards.

As soon as the court deputy let go of Dylan's arm, Dylan turned around and gave me the biggest smile he could muster up. He was so happy. And so was I, because my man was finally getting out of jail.

"Next case," I heard the judge say, which was my cue to exit the courtroom.

While I was leaving the courtroom, I saw a guy walking near me through my peripheral vision. I turned around casually, and what do you know, Detective Grimes was following at my heels. I instantly got a bad taste in my mouth so I turned around to confront him. "What the hell do you want now?" I asked him sarcastically.

He gave me a smirk that irritated the crap out of me. "I'm just amazed at the lengths you'd go to help your boyfriend get his case dismissed."

"All I did was get him the best attorney money could buy."

"Oh, you did more than that. And one day soon I'll be able to prove it," Detective Grimes said, and then he turned around and walked off.

I was so shocked by his statement that I couldn't say another word. I just stood there in awe, wondering how I was going to stay a couple of steps ahead of him. I mean, this guy had it out for me. He made me feel like he hated my guts. So, I could never let him see me slipping because if I did, then I might as well kiss my freedom goodbye.

Chapter 33

It's Not Over!

I took a seat on one of the benches outside of the courtroom after the run-in I had with Detective Grimes. I can't lie, this freaking guy had me on edge. The thought of him solving my father's murder made me feel sick to my stomach. I couldn't allow that to happen because that would send me to prison for the rest of my life. And I wasn't strong enough mentally to spend the rest of my life in prison. No way. My life would be spent out here on these streets and I was going to make sure that that happened.

It took a few hours before the jail released Dylan. I was told by Mr. Berlinsky to meet him outside the gates near the visitors' entrance of the jail, so I did. And the moment I laid eyes on Dylan, I was instantly filled up with emotions and started crying. I raced towards him and jumped into his arms. I wrapped my legs around his waist and started kissing him passionately. "I love you so much!" I said after I kissed him four consecutive times.

"I love you too, baby. And now that I'm out of that joint," he said, pointing towards the jail, "I'm gonna make sure I take good care of you. I'm handling everything from this point on, okay?" he replied as he cupped my ass cheeks with both of his hands.

"Okay," I said with a smile. And then it quickly dawned on me that I was acting like the late Whitney Houston acted when she jumped into Bobby Brown's arms after he was released from jail. I swear, it felt good to be in my man's arms again and I didn't want this moment to end.

After holding me for what felt like a little over one minute, he released me so I could stand on my feet. I stood there before him so I could get a good look at him. "You're so cute, but you need a haircut, baby," I commented in a joking manner.

He smiled. "Don't worry about it. I'm gonna get that taken care of right after you take me to see my mother."

"Well, let's go," I said.

"All right, then come on," Dylan replied. He grabbed my hand and we walked hand in hand right up to the moment we reached my car. Like always, Dylan opened the car door for me and after I got inside he closed the door behind me.

Immediately after he got into the passenger seat, he closed the door and that's when I pulled off into the sunset. I think the fresh air was doing Dylan some good because, for the first couple of minutes in the car, he rolled down the passenger-side window and laid his head against the headrest, and closed his eyes. I knew he was in deep thought so I didn't bother him.

It was my idea to call his mother before we drove over to her place. Unfortunately for us, she didn't answer her cell phone. So, then we called Sonya's cell phone number. She didn't answer her phone either. *You reached the right person, but at the wrong time. Leave me a message at the sound of the beep.* BEEP!

"Why the fuck aren't they answering their phones?" Dylan asked me. He sounded aggravated.

"Sonya texted me back the other day saying that she's working double shifts. And your mother is probably taking a nap or at church. She told me not too long ago that she's been volunteering at the daycare center the church just opened," I tried to explain.

"I'd rather see her doing anything but sitting at the house with that coward-ass husband of hers," Dylan commented.

"Yeah, me too," I agreed while I watched Dylan dial Nick's cell phone number from my phone.

I heard his cell phone ring twice before he answered it. "You better be calling and telling me that they let my homeboy out!" Nick expressed with excitement.

"Come on, man, you know they couldn't keep me forever!" Dylan bragged.

"Kira wasn't having it either way."

"Yeah, she held me down," Dylan acknowledged. "So, where you at?"

"I'm at Bianca's crib. Why, what's up?"

"Well, I'm on my way to my mom's house. But after I leave there, I wanna get with you so you can bring me up to speed about what's been going on with our investments."

"Oh yeah, let's do that. Meet me at my crib at eight o'clock tonight," I heard Nick say to Dylan.

"A'ight, see you then," Dylan replied.

⟹●⟸

Dylan and I arrived at his mother's house in twenty-five minutes. Bruce's car was parked in the driveway but Mrs. Daisy's car wasn't, so Dylan and I automatically assumed that she was spending her time at the church volunteering in the daycare center. But we wanted to make sure, so he got out of the car and knocked on the front door. Surprisingly, Bruce opened it. He kept the glass storm door closed, though. I rolled down the car window so I could hear what they were saying.

"Hey, Bruce, what's up?" Dylan started off.

"Nothing much, what can I do for you?" he wanted to know.

"I wanna see my mother. So, where is she?"

"She's not here."

"I can see that. So, tell me where I can find her."

"She's with your sister," he replied in an unconcerned manner.

"How long have they been gone?"

"I'm not sure. Maybe two hours."

"Did she say where she and Sonya were going?"

"Nope," Bruce said coldly.

"Does she have her cell phone with her?"

"I'm sure she does."

"So, how is everything going on with you and my mother?"

"Everything is going well."

"Well, I heard differently."

"Whatever you heard is a lie."

"Look, Bruce, I didn't come over here to get in an argument with you. I just wanna see my mother. That's it."

"Well, she's not here."

"Tell her to call me when she gets in. And if I don't hear from her by nightfall I'm coming back over here, okay?"

"You can do whatever you want to," Bruce said nonchalantly as he continued to stand in the doorway of the house, with the storm door separating them. It seemed like everything Dylan said to him went in one ear and out of the other.

This pissed Dylan off. He took one step closer to the storm door and said, "Come on, Bruce, why you gotta be a smart-ass? I'm trying to be civilized with you and you're trying to make this shit hard."

"Are you done?" Bruce asked sarcastically. And from the expression he gave Dylan, I knew shit was about to hit the fan, so I hopped out of my car and rushed over to the front porch.

By the time I got within three feet of Dylan, he had taken another step towards the storm door. "Listen, you fucking coward, cause I'm gonna only say this one more time: If my mother doesn't call me back when she gets back, I'm gonna come over here and you and I are going to have a man-to-man conversation. Do you understand me?" Dylan roared. I could see his veins bulging in his neck. I grabbed him by the arm and tried to pull him back towards me.

"Dylan, come on, baby, he's not worth it," I said.

"You better listen to your girlfriend," Bruce advised Dylan. Now, this set Dylan off. "Whatcha just say to me, loser?" Dylan barked.

"I said, you better listen to your girlfriend," Bruce replied calmly, but in a cynical manner.

I saw Dylan reach for the doorknob, so I grabbed his wrist and snatched it back. "Dylan, let's go right now," I pleaded. Dylan resisted a little. "Dylan, let's go and wait for your mom to call you," I continued while I held on to his hand.

Finally, after four attempts to get Dylan to listen to me, he stopped resisting and allowed me to pull him away from the glass door. "You better have her call me before the night is over," Dylan warned Bruce again as he exited the porch. Bruce didn't utter another word. Instead, he closed the front door, and then I heard him lock it.

Immediately after we got back into my car, Dylan started cursing and talking about how badly he wanted to snatch the storm door off the hinges and beat Bruce's ass. "Kira, I swear I hate that fucking guy! And you have no idea how badly I wanna kill that coward with my bare hands! I wanna snatch away his last breath!" he roared as he sat forward on the passenger side of my car.

I listened to him vent while I drove away from his mother's house. "Calm down, baby! He's a miserable old man. Trust me, he's gonna get what's coming to him," I expressed.

Chapter 34

Playtime Is Over

Dylan called his barber to get an appointment. Thankfully, the barber told him to come right over and he'd take care of him. Instead of going inside of the barbershop and waiting for Dylan to get his haircut, I elected to wait outside in the car. I needed to clear my head, and sitting in a barbershop with a bunch of men running their mouths about women, the economy, and other nonsense wasn't how I wanted to spend the rest of my day. Trying to figure out my next move was what I needed to focus on. I couldn't say how long that was going to take, but the sooner I did it, the sooner I could stop being paranoid and looking over my shoulder every time I left my apartment. If it wasn't Kendrick or his boys watching me, it was that wannabe super cop Detective Grimes. I wished everyone would just leave me alone already. Ugh!

While I was waiting for Dylan to get his haircut, I got a phone call from Eric, my contact guy down at Dexter's Funeral Home. I put the call on speaker after I answered it. "Hi, Eric," I said. Eric didn't know it, but I started feeling uneasy with this conversation we were about to have.

"Hi, Kira," he replied. "So, I'm calling you to let you know that your father's body is ready and that we're setting his body out tonight in room 4 for his viewing, which will start at nine a.m. tomorrow."

"Are we still having his funeral service at noon?" I asked him.

"Yes, we are. It's gonna start on time at the Roosevelt Cemetery."

"How long will the service be?"

"Well, since you aren't expecting a huge crowd, the service could take as little as thirty minutes, unless you wanna stick around and watch the groundskeepers lower his casket into the ground and cover it with dirt."

"No, I don't wanna see that. That will just tear me apart," I expressed. I've lied about a lot of things, but I wasn't lying about how I would be affected seeing the groundskeepers putting my father's body in the ground. He was being buried because I murdered him. So, there's no way I was going to allow guilt to ride me worse than what it was doing to me now. I couldn't allow it to happen.

"Okay, well, that's fine. You're entitled to mourn your loved one the way you see fit. So, I'm gonna go for now. But if you need anything else, call the office and either myself or my sister will take care of you," he assured me.

"Thank you so much," I replied, and then we ended our call.

⸻

Dylan's haircut appointment seemed like it took forever. So, when he walked back out to the car, I was resting my head back against the headrest with my eyes closed. He startled me when he grabbed the car door handle. I sat straight up, trying to focus my eyes on what had just happened. When I realized it was Dylan trying to get back into the car, I unlocked the car door. "You just scared the shit out of me!" I told him after I gasped.

"Baby, I'm sorry," he said while he was getting back into the car. After he closed the door, he kissed me on the cheek.

"It's okay," I said while I started up the ignition.

Dylan started massaging my right shoulder while I drove towards the main road. "You got a lot of pressure going on in this area," he stated as he glanced over at me.

"I've got a lot of pressure in other places too," I added.

"Well, I'm gonna relieve you of all of it. From now on, I don't want you stressing out about anything. I'm home now, so I'm gonna take care of everything," Dylan promised me. I didn't mention it to him, but I loved when he took charge of everything, leaving me with absolutely nothing to worry about. I loved that about him. Dylan has been the best thing that has ever happened to me. Hands down!

"I just got off the phone with a guy named Eric from the funeral home," I announced.

"What did he say?" Dylan wanted to know.

"He wanted me to know that my father's body was ready and that he'll be put in one of the rooms at the funeral home by morning. That way, if anyone wants to stop by there to see him before the service starts at noon then they'd be able to," I explained.

"How do you feel?" Dylan asked. He seemed concerned.

"Baby, I don't know anymore."

"Have you thought about what's going to happen with your father's house?"

"No. I haven't thought about it."

"Do you have a relative somewhere that you can call to come down here to help you?" Dylan wanted to know.

"Not really. The ones I do have left are distant second and third cousins. And I haven't seen any of them since I went to a family reunion about fifteen years ago. I told you my family was small," I replied nonchalantly.

"Does he have a life insurance policy?"

"Yeah, he has one."

"You're the beneficiary, right?"

"I'm sure I am."

"So, you haven't called to check?"

"No, I haven't," I replied. His constant questions were irritating me.

"Well, who's paying for the funeral?"

"I am," I told him. "And don't worry, I'm using my own money," I added. I wanted Dylan to be aware that I wasn't using any of his money, given the circumstances that my father was the reason why he was in jail.

"It's not about whose money you're using. I just wanna make sure you call the insurance company, because they aren't gonna reach out to you. They'd rather not pay the claim at all," he enlightened me.

"I'll call them after the funeral," I said. "Here, take my phone and call Sonya. See if she'll answer her phone now." I handed him my cell phone.

"I know what you're doing by telling me to call Sonya," he said as he took my cell phone from my hand. I didn't say another word. But he was right. He knew I wanted to get off the subject of my father's funeral. The only thing he didn't know was why I wanted to switch the subject. As badly as I wanted to tell him what I had done, right now wasn't the time.

I watched him through my peripheral vision as he dialed his sister's cell phone number. But before the phone could ring, her voicemail message played. Dylan hadn't turned on the speakerphone function but I could still hear it. *You reached the right person, but at the wrong time. Leave me a message at the sound of the beep.* BEEP!

"Leave her a message," I whispered to him.

"Hey, sis, you know who it is. Hit me and Kira up. We're trying to see you and Mama," Dylan said and then he disconnected the call.

"Wanna drive over to her house? If she's with your mother then they gotta be at her house, especially with all the shit Bruce has been putting her through," I suggested.

"What shit?" Dylan asked. He completely caught me off guard. I had forgotten to tell him that Bruce had been physically abusing Mrs. Daisy.

"Baby, don't be mad at me . . ." I started off saying.

"What happened, Kira?" he asked me, already sounding angry and I hadn't opened my mouth to say anything yet.

"Sonya called me a week ago and told me that Bruce was at their house beating on your mother. So, Nick and I rode over there to check things out but Bruce wouldn't let us in the house. And when we called Sonya back to see where she was, she didn't answer her phone, so we left. I figured that one of them would call when they wanted me to come back over there."

"Are you fucking kidding me right now?!" Dylan roared. I could see his eyes turn bloodshot red. "That fucking coward put his hands on my mother and you're just now telling me?" he continued.

"Baby, I'm sorry. But you were locked up when it happened. You were already dealing with the charges because of my dad, so why stress you out even more? I mean, it's not like you could've done something about it. You were in jail, for heaven's sake."

"It shouldn't have mattered where I was. Anything going on with my family, I wanna know about it. Simple as that. Now, turn this motherfucking car around and take me back to my mother's house. I'm gonna straighten that clown out once and for all," Dylan barked.

"I'm not taking you back over there so you can catch another charge. Are you fucking crazy?!" I barked back.

"When it comes to my mother, do you think I care about

getting another charge? I will kill that bitch-ass coward with my bare hands!" he roared.

"I know you will. That's why we're not going back over there. We're going over to Sonya's house, so hopefully, they are there. And if they are, then we can convince your mother to come back to the house with us. Deal?" I replied, trying to compromise with him.

"Nah, fuck that! Take me back to my mom's crib, Kira. I ain't gonna be able to live with myself if I don't deal with that motherfucker now!" Dylan said while he was rocking himself back and forth in the seat next to me. From the way things were looking, he wasn't going to let this thing go.

I pulled my car over to the side of the road and immediately after I put the gear in park, I turned around and faced Dylan. "Baby, please listen to me," I began to say. "If we go to your mother's house right now, Bruce is going to call the cops on you, no questions asked. Now, do you want to risk your freedom again? Look at it this way—you haven't been out of jail for twenty-four hours and you're making waves to go back inside. I can't let you do that. I need you out here with me," I continued while I gave him the sincerest expression I could muster up.

Dylan sat there for a moment. I could tell that he was fighting with trying to make a decision. So I sat there and waited for him to break his silence.

"I'll tell you what, if you take me by my mom's house and I don't see her car parked outside, then I won't go up to the front door," he proposed.

"Why go over there when she's probably at Sonya's place?" I countered.

"We just called Sonya and she didn't answer her phone. So, they may not even be there, which is why I'd rather ride back over to my mom's house. There's a possibility that she could be there by now," Dylan replied.

I sat there unable to say another word. Dylan was making it abundantly clear that he was going back to his mother's house and that was it. So I let him win this one and turned back around in my seat. After I put my gearshift in drive, I pulled back onto the road and headed in the direction of Mrs. Daisy's house.

Chapter 35

What Did I Get Myself Into?

Dylan and I didn't say another word to each other the entire drive back to his mother's house. And even though I was quiet, I was praying silently the whole way there. I asked God to take control of this situation. I didn't want Dylan going back to jail. I needed him home with me. I couldn't continue to go head-to-head with Detective Grimes and Kendrick alone. I needed Dylan with me to ward off those evil-ass men because sooner or later something more tragic than my dad dying was going to happen.

Immediately after I drove onto Mrs. Daisy's street, Dylan sat up in the seat when we saw a car backing out of the driveway of his mother's house. It was dark outside, but we could still see the shape of the back of the car and the taillights. "Hurry up, that looks like my mother's car," Dylan said in an urgent manner.

I pressed down on the accelerator and sped towards Mrs. Daisy's house. From the looks of it, we were finally going to see her. Optimism filled my entire body while I was pulling up near the entryway of the driveway. Before I could bring my car to a complete stop, Dylan hopped out of the passenger-side door. I watched him as he walked around the front of my car while I struggled to put the gear in park. I jumped out of the driver's seat a few seconds later. "You are just the person I want to see," I heard Dylan say after I closed the driver-side door. And when I took a couple of steps towards the car, I realized it was Bruce's car and he was driving it. My heart dropped and all of the optimism and excitement I had inside of me quickly deflated. "Bruce, roll down the window so I can talk to you. As a matter of fact, get out of the car so we can have a man-to-man conversation," Dylan demanded as he pulled on the door handle a couple of times.

I couldn't hear a word Bruce was saying, but I saw his mouth moving. And I saw how carefully he was trying to back out of the driveway without rolling over Dylan and me. At one point, it sounded like he was warning Dylan to move out of the way before he rolled over the top of us, but Dylan ignored Bruce. So, Bruce pressed down the accelerator and backed out of the driveway as quickly as he could without losing control. Dylan jumped into action and raced towards Bruce's car. "No, Dylan, don't . . ." I yelled, hoping he wouldn't do anything crazy like jump on the hood of the car or punch the windows out with his fists.

"You wanna put your hands on my mama? I am going to murder your ass tonight!" Dylan yelled as he scrambled to get as close to the car as quickly as possible. I scurried behind him in hopes to stop him from doing something he would later regret. "Don't run, you fucking coward!" Dylan huffed and started kicking the driver's-side door with his feet.

"No, Dylan, let him go!" I yelled. Thankfully Bruce was able to put his car in drive, and sped off before Dylan could get close to him to do any major damage.

I stood there trying to catch my breath while I watched Bruce drive away from the house. But that all went up in smoke when I noticed Dylan getting into the driver's seat of my car. "Where are you going with my car?" I yelled while I ran back towards my car.

"I'm going to get that motherfucker! So, come on!" he roared.

I knew there was no way I could talk to him standing outside the car, so I hopped in the passenger seat and immediately started pleading with him. "Babe, what are you doing? You gotta stop before we both get arrested," I warned him.

"Fuck that! I'm gonna kill that motherfucker tonight," Dylan protested as he sped off behind Bruce's car.

"Dylan, you can't do that. Remember, we didn't come here for that. You promised me . . ." I pleaded with him while I was still facing him.

"He hit my mama, Kira. I can't let that go."

"I know, Dylan. But getting him this way is only gonna put you back in jail. And I need you out here because . . ." And then I fell silent and started crying.

Dylan finally turned his attention towards me and slowed the car down. "Because what?" he asked me. I turned around in the seat and faced forward. "Pull the car over at that stop sign," I instructed him while I pointed to a stop sign half a block away. We were still in his mother's neighborhood, so I felt like this would be a better place than any to break the news to him about my father's murder. The streets were quiet and from what I could see, there weren't any suspicious-looking cars following us. Surprisingly Dylan pulled over and parked the car. I got out of the car and he followed me. "Tell me what's going on," he didn't hesitate to say.

I grabbed him and pulled him close to me. And I leaned in towards him, targeting the cheek area of his face so I could talk quietly in his ear. "I was the one that killed my father," I started off by saying, and when I tried to tell him more, he grabbed both of my arms and pushed me back a little without letting me go.

"You did what?" he said, his words barely audible.

"I did it for you. I got Nick to take me to my dad's house, we drove him to an empty lot, I shot him and then I set the truck on fire."

"Who else knows about this?"

"Kendrick knows."

"How the fuck did he find out before me?" Dylan spat.

"I don't know. He saw me at the gas station two days ago and told me that he heard what I did. I tried to deny it, but he didn't believe me."

"You know he's gonna hold that over your head, right?"

"Come on now, you know I'm not stupid."

"Well, don't worry about him. He's already on my hit list. I'm gonna make sure he never bothers you again."

Dylan pulled me back towards him and then he embraced me. He held me so tight, it felt like he was never gonna let me go. "Oh my God! Kira, I am so sorry you had to do that for me," he whispered in my ear.

"I did it because I love you," I told him as I began to cry. And when Dylan heard me sobbing, he held me even tighter.

"I love you too, baby. And I promise I will never let anyone else separate us again," he promised me.

"Okay," I replied while the tears continued to fall from my eyes.

Dylan and I stood near the stop sign for a few more minutes and then we got back into the car. By now, Dylan was no longer concerned about hurting Bruce. After the news I had just given him, he was more concerned about me than anything else. "Come on, let's go home," he started off. "Nah, I think we should wait for Sonya or my mama to call us back," he continued and then we headed back to my car.

196 / KIKI SWINSON

"All right," I agreed.

It felt good to finally tell Dylan my secret. I swear it felt like a burden was lifted from me. Now, all we needed to concentrate on was getting past my father's funeral and getting Mrs. Daisy away from Bruce before he hurt her badly and Dylan ended up back in prison. I guess Dylan and I had some work to do.

———◈◈———

When Dylan and I got back to our apartment we ate the food we picked up from a Chinese spot two blocks from our house. Not much longer after we devoured our food, Dylan carried me to our bedroom and fucked my brains out. I had to admit that the lovemaking session we had was far overdue.

While we were in bed trying to go to sleep, Dylan wanted me to know that he planned to stop over at Sonya's house right after we leave my father's funeral since she didn't call us back. I told him that would be fine. At this point, whatever he felt was best for us, that was how things would be.

Chapter 36

Ashes to Ashes,
Dust to Dust

I couldn't believe how tired I was until I woke up this morning not wanting to get out of bed. Today was the day I was burying my father, but I couldn't come to terms with the fact that I wasn't going to see him again. For some odd reason, it felt like I was having a bad dream and that I was going to wake up from it at any given moment.

I was standing in front of the vanity connected to my bathroom sink, looking at myself. In just a little over a week, it looked like I'd aged at least ten years. I had black circles around my eyes and my cheeks looked like they were sunken in.

Dylan walked up behind me and wrapped his arms around my waist. "Why aren't you dressed? You know the funeral starts in two hours," he reminded me.

"Don't worry, I'm gonna be ready on time," I told him.

Dylan kissed me on the back of my neck. "You know I love you, right?" he whispered into my ear.

I looked at him through the mirror in front of us. "Yes, I do," I replied, and then I mustered up a smile.

He moved back from me and smacked me on the butt and said, "Well, hurry up and get ready. We've got a lot of stuff to do today." Then he exited the bathroom.

I stood there for a few more minutes thinking about how I was going to react when I finally walked into the room where my father's body was being held. Was I going to continue to feel guilty or was I going to feel like my actions were justified? Either way, I knew I was going to have some strong feelings. I guess I had to walk into that room to see which one was going to outpower the other.

Once I had gotten dressed in all-black funeral attire, I put on my dark sunshades, grabbed my purse and my car keys, and Dylan and I left the apartment. Instead of taking my car, we decided to take his. The valet attendants had his car in front of the building when we walked outside. "It's good to see you, sir," one of the valets announced to Dylan. "Yeah, it's been a while, huh?" Dylan commented as he handed the guy a twenty-dollar bill while another valet driver helped me into the passenger seat.

Immediately after our doors were closed Dylan drove away from the curb. "Think they've been talking about us?" Dylan asked me.

"I'm sure they have," I replied while I stared out of the passenger-side window.

"You gotta point there," he commented, and then he fell silent. A few minutes later he sparked up another conversation. "Don't forget I said that we're gonna stop by Sonya's house after we leave the cemetery."

"Yes, I remember."

"Good. Hopefully, my mama is there too."

"I can't see why she wouldn't be," I said while I continued to stare out of the window. But really, I couldn't care less what we did after we left the funeral. My main focus right now was getting through the funeral service. I only had enough energy inside of me for that chapter in my life. Everything else meant nothing to me right now.

It seemed like the closer we got to the funeral home, the heavier my anxiety felt. I was a ball of nerves, to put it mildly.

And I couldn't tell you how long I would feel this way. But I prayed it would be over sooner than later.

Dylan and I arrived at the funeral home twenty minutes after we left our apartment. And after he let me out of the car, he and I walked hand in hand through the front entrance. We were greeted by Eric and Gina Dexter. They were brother and sister and the son and daughter of the founders of the funeral home. They were also appointed to handle the service for my father. "How was the drive here?" Eric asked us.

"It was fairly easy," Dylan told them.

"Great, I'm glad," Eric replied.

"So, are you guys ready?" Gina asked with a sympathetic expression.

I wanted to answer her but my mouth wouldn't open so I gave her a head nod.

"Well, let me inform you that there are a few of your father's friends in the room viewing his body. So, we told them that as soon as you arrived that we were going to start the service," Gina stated.

Hearing her tell me that my father had friends in the other room viewing his body kind of caught me off guard because he didn't have a lot of friends. Judge Mahoney and his wife were like best friends and that was pretty much it. Now, he did have a few former colleagues that he used to play golf with, but that was over a decade ago. So to label themselves friends seemed to be a little odd to me. "How many people are actually in that room?" I finally was able to speak.

"There's a total of maybe five," she replied as she searched my face for a reaction. "Is everything all right?" she asked me.

"Yes, everything is fine," I responded nonchalantly. Truth be told, everything wasn't fine. I wanted to know who was in that room before I walked in there. I don't like surprises at all.

"Are you sure, baby? Because I can go and check things out while you stay right here."

"No, I'm fine. Let's get this over with," I told him and then I turned my attention towards Eric and Gina.

"Well, I guess you can follow us," Eric said, and then he led the way to the room where my father's service was being held.

The knots in my stomach started twisting and turning as we started walking towards the service area. At one point, it felt like my knees were going to buckle underneath me. Thankfully, Dylan held on to my arm the entire time.

Immediately after we entered the room, all eyes turned their attention towards me. I recognized all five of the people sitting in chairs near my father's casket. Three of them were judges, one of which had denied Dylan's bail at his hearing. The other two judges were close to my father. The female of the bunch had worked as his courtroom clerk. Her name was Sandy Taylor. She was a young Hispanic woman who looked to be in her mid to late forties. I remember how my dad used to talk about how loyal she was and how great her work performance was. So, I walked over to her and thanked her for attending his farewell service. The three judges turned their heads. They sent me a clear message that they weren't interested in talking to me, so Dylan and I continued in the direction of a set of chairs to the left of my father's casket.

The last person I recognized amongst the others was the prosecutor that played a heavy role in getting Dylan's bail denied. I wanted to give him a piece of my mind, but I figured now wouldn't be a good time. We were supposed to be here celebrating my father's homegoing, and that's how it was going to be.

Once Dylan and I sat down, the chapel's minister came from the back room and the service started. "We are here today to seek and to receive comfort," he started off. "We would be less than honest if we said that our hearts have not ached over this situation. We are not too proud to acknowledge that we have come here today trusting that God would minister to our hearts, and give us strength as we continue in our walk with Him. It is our human nature to want to understand everything now, but trust requires that we lean and rely heavily on God even when things seem unclear," he continued. He even bragged about how nice my father was and how much the community loved him, which was a damn lie. The minister rambled on for another twenty-five minutes about how great my dad was and how he was in a better place. Then he started talking about how tomorrow isn't promised to us so we need to seek a personal relationship with God. The service was so emotional it felt like we were in church. And when he began the closing prayer to end the service, it tore my heart in two. I wanted to run up to my father's casket and fall to my knees and pour my heart out to him. I wanted to tell him I was sorry. But I knew that wouldn't have been a good idea. Every one of my father's former peers would have me arrested on the spot.

When the prayer was finally over, the minister thanked everyone for attending my father's service and then he dismissed us. Now, when friends attend a funeral arranged by one of the family members, they would normally give their condolences, but not this handful of assholes. Every single one of those people left without saying *goodbye*, *kiss my ass*, or *fuck you*. They didn't even look in my direction after they marched out of the funeral home. They eyed me down when I first walked into the room. But now that the service was over, they wouldn't even acknowledge me. I say to hell with all of them. Rude motherfuckers!

The funeral officials loaded my father's casket into the hearse while Dylan and I got into his car. I assumed that the other judges, the prosecutor, and my father's former courtroom clerk were going to follow us to the cemetery, but they drove off in the opposite direction when the driver of the hearse drove away from the funeral home. Dylan noticed it too. "So, I guess it's just you and I going to the cemetery," Dylan commented.

"I guess so," I replied without the slightest care in the world.

"I can't believe that the same prosecutor that tried to railroad my ass in court was there."

"I don't know why not. It wouldn't surprise me if all of them showed up to spy on us."

"If that's the case, we should've given them something to talk about."

"Nah, we acted like we were supposed to."

"How do you think the minister did at the service?"

"I guess he did all right. I mean, I wasn't listening to him. I couldn't stop looking at my dad's casket," I said while I stared out of the passenger-side window.

Dylan massaged the back of my neck the entire drive to the cemetery and I have to admit that the touch of his hand made me feel better than I had before I walked into the funeral home over an hour ago. I knew Dylan loved me. I also believed that he was going to make things better too. Crossing that hurdle would be somewhat complicated, but I figured once that part was over, then I'd be home free.

When we arrived at the cemetery, the minister got out of the passenger side of the hearse and walked with Dylan and me to the burial site. A few minutes later, two of the funeral home officials rolled my father's casket from the hearse to the burial site too. Dylan and I stood there and bowed our heads for another round of prayer. And when the minister closed the prayer with "In Jesus's name," I lifted my head, blew a kiss at my father's casket, and then I turned around and walked back to Dylan's car. I swear I couldn't get out of that cemetery fast enough. Being surrounded by a bunch of dead bodies gave me an eerie feeling. Thank God Dylan was on the same page as me. I didn't have to tell him that I was ready to go, he already knew it.

Chapter 37

No More Bad News!

As Dylan drove away from the cemetery, Nick called Dylan to confirm a meeting they were having later. "Kira and I just left the funeral and now we're on our way to Sonya's house. So as soon as I drop Kira back off to our apartment, I'll head over there," I heard Dylan say. After Nick agreed to the time of the meeting, they ended their call.

⇒►◄⇐

Upon entering the Coral Gables neighborhood where Sonya lived, Dylan stated that he and his sister were going to find a way to get Bruce out of his mother's house. "Don't you think my attorney could help me with that?" he asked me as we cruised through the neighborhood.

"I don't see why not," I stated without looking at him.

"Well, I hope so, because he's gotta go. I can't have anyone putting their hands on anyone I love. That's unacceptable," Dylan started off, and then he paused. "Hey, wait, I don't see Sonya's car."

I turned my attention towards a row of town houses and noticed that Dylan was right. Sonya's car wasn't parked outside of her town house. "Think she might be at work?" Dylan asked me.

"She could be," I replied.

"Do you have the number to her job?" he asked me as he pulled into a parking space directly in front of her town house.

"I think so," I told him and then I grabbed my cell phone from my purse. I searched my contact list and found a phone number for Sonya's job. I dialed it and waited for someone to answer. Immediately after I heard a woman say, "Thank you for calling Assisted Living, how can I help you?" I pressed the speakerphone function button so Dylan could hear the conversation.

"Hi, my name is Kira and I'm looking for Sonya Callender-Morris. I'm her sister-in-law and I've been trying to contact her for the last couple of days with virtually no luck. So I was wondering if I could speak with her for a minute or so if she's available?"

"I'm sorry, ma'am, but Sonya hasn't been to work in over a week now. We've been trying to contact her ourselves," the woman stated.

"What does she mean she hasn't been to work?" Dylan blurted out.

"Ma'am, are you sure?" I asked. I instantly became sick to my stomach. I couldn't fathom Sonya missing work. Was she all right?

"Yes, I'm positive. I've sent one of my staff members over to her place after the third day and they left a note on her door letting her know that we were worried about her and that she needed to give us a call."

"Oh my God! This can't be," I said while I stared into Dylan's eyes, but at the same time trying to figure out where in the hell Sonya could be.

"My name is Amy Glass. When you get a chance to speak with her, let her know that she needs to give us a call."

"I most certainly will," I assured the woman and then I ended the call.

"What the fuck is going on?" Dylan cursed. I could see the veins in his temple flaring up.

"Do you think this has something to do with Bruce? I mean, what if he has her and your mother tied up in the basement of that house?" I asked suspiciously.

"I'm telling you right now, if that motherfucker touched a hair on my mother's or sister's head, no one is gonna stop me from killing him."

"Baby, let's not think the worst. There's gotta be a good explanation why Sonya hasn't been to work. So, let's start here."

"What do you mean?"

"You gotta spare key to her place, right?"

"Yeah."

"Well, let's go inside and check things out. Who knows, maybe she left town without telling us."

Without saying another word Dylan exited the car. I followed him. After Dylan figured out which key on his key ring belonged to Sonya's place, he unlocked the front door and then we let ourselves in. A stale smell hit me in the nose instantly as I walked down the hallway. It wasn't an odor indicating that there was a corpse in the house, so I was fine with it.

From the looks of things, nothing seemed out of place. The kitchen was spotless and so was the living room. "She keeps a pretty clean house," I pointed out as I scanned both rooms. Dylan didn't comment. Instead, he stepped away from me and headed in the direction of Sonya's bedroom. I followed suit.

As soon as we entered Sonya's bedroom we noticed that her bed hadn't been made. But still, nothing was out of place that suggested something had happened to her. "Check her closet," Dylan instructed me while he searched underneath her bed.

"I'm on it," I told him and marched over to her walk-in closet. When I opened the door, I noticed that her favorite suitcase that she used every time she left town was tucked away next to a box where she kept her hats. This wasn't a good sign. "Baby, I don't think Sonya left town," I spoke up.

Dylan stood on his feet. "What do you mean?" he asked me as he walked towards me.

I grabbed her favorite suitcase and pulled it out of the closet. "She never leaves town without this suitcase. It's her favorite. So, I think we should call the police," I said.

"Wait, let me call her one more time first," Dylan replied, and then he pulled his cell phone out and dialed Sonya's cell phone number. Once again the voicemail message played before the phone could ring. *You reached the right person, but at the wrong time. Leave me a message at the sound of the beep.* BEEP!

Dylan cleared the line and dialed Sonya's cell phone number again. The voicemail message played again. *You reached the right person, but at the wrong time. Leave me a message at the sound of the beep.* BEEP!

"I'm calling the cops," I announced. I took my cell phone out of my purse and dialed 911. "This is 911, what's your emergency?" a female dispatcher asked.

"Umm, I want to report a missing person. Her name is Sonya Callender-Morris and we believe that she's been missing for over a week now."

"How do you know she's been missing for over a week?"

"Because that's the last time we spoke to her. And the people at her job say that she hasn't been to work for the same period of time," I explained.

"How old is she?" the operator asked.

"She's thirty."

"Is she married or single?"

"She's married. But her husband has been deployed to Afghanistan."

"Have you been to her house?"

"Her brother and I are here now. We have a spare key to her home."

"What's the address to that residence?"

"It's 301 Madeira Avenue."

"Okay, well, sit tight. I just dispatched a unit so they should be there soon."

"Thank you," I said and then I ended the call. "Come on, let's wait for them outside," I continued, and then I walked towards the front door. Dylan followed me without saying anything.

Chapter 38

Missing Persons

Two police officers, white males, showed up at Sonya's house about ten minutes later. Dylan and I met them on the front porch. The officers introduced themselves as Officer Towson and Officer Vass and then they started asking Dylan and me a long list of questions about Sonya. "So, you say she's been missing for over a week?" Officer Vass asked.

"Yes," I replied.

"Do you think she could've left town?" he continued.

"No, she's very close with us. She would tell us if she had to leave. Not only that, she loves her job and we just found out a few minutes ago that she hasn't been there in over a week."

"Have you tried contacting her on her cell phone?"

"We've been trying to call her for the last couple of days but her phone goes straight to voicemail. We've also been trying to get in touch with my mother. We think they might be together," Dylan interjected.

"So, your mother lives here too?" Officer Towson asked.

"No, she lives across town with her new abusive husband. He's been keeping us from seeing my mother too."

"So, you're saying that your mother is missing too?" the same officer asked.

"I'm not sure. My fiancée and I have been over there a few times, but her husband keeps telling us that she's not there, that she's with my sister. I think he's got them held hostage in my mom's house," Dylan added.

"Don't say that, Dylan, you don't know that for sure," I blurted out.

"What's the address to your mother's residence?" Officer Vass asked.

"I don't know it, but I can show you where it is," Dylan offered.

"Okay, but let us take a look around your sister's place, and then we'll follow you guys to your mother's house," Officer Vass replied.

"All right, well, we'll wait out here until you're done," I told him.

"Good. We will be right back," Officer Vass said and then they went into Sonya's house.

After they disappeared into the house I turned towards Dylan. "Why would you tell them that Bruce may have them held hostage?"

"Where else can they be, Kira? They aren't here. And didn't he tell us that they were together?"

"Yes, but—" I began, but Dylan cut me off in midsentence.

"But, nothing . . . He knows where they are and if he doesn't tell me, I'm gonna kill him."

"You're gonna kill who?" Officer Towson asked when he reemerged from Sonya's house.

"I'm talking about my mother's husband." Dylan repeated himself without hesitating.

"He doesn't mean that. He's just venting because he's frustrated," I interjected.

Officer Towson didn't say another word. He did give Dylan a bizarre-looking facial expression. "So, are y'all ready to head over to his mother's house?" I continued, trying to lighten the mood.

"As soon as my partner comes out, we will leave," the same officer replied.

"Well, we're gonna wait in the car until he does," Dylan said.

"Wouldn't it be a good idea to lock the front door after my partner comes out?" the officer asked.

"He can lock it from the inside and then close the door," Dylan instructed.

"I'll make sure he does that," Officer Towson assured us.

Dylan and I climbed back into his car and waited for the other officer to come back out of Sonya's house. He resurfaced a few minutes later. Officer Towson instructed Officer Vass to lock the front door from the inside and then they both got into their squad car.

Dylan backed out of the parking space we were in and then we headed in the direction of his mother's house. The ride was smooth but the thought of two cops following us seemed kind of weird. "Think they ran your license plate?" I asked.

"I couldn't care less. Finding my sister is way more important than cops trying to find out who I am," he replied sarcastically.

"If Bruce is at the house, do you think he's going to let us in?" I wondered aloud.

"That's my father's house, so he better let me in," Dylan hissed.

"Baby, listen. I know you wanna tear that asshole in half, but you gotta be careful about how you act and what you say around the cops. You don't want them hauling your ass back downtown," I warned him.

"I don't give a damn about that!" he huffed.

I pinched his thigh. "Dylan, you promised me." I reminded

him about not leaving me out here on the streets again while he's in jail.

"Well, just keep that moron away from me," Dylan urged.

"Don't worry, I will," I assured him.

———⇒◦⇐———

Dylan pulled his car curbside in front of his mother's house, while the officers parked their vehicle directly behind Bruce's car. Once again, there was no sign of Mrs. Daisy's car, which worried me.

"Do you want us to go up to the house with you?" Dylan yelled from the car window.

"We'd prefer if you'd stay in the car," Officer Vass replied.

Ignoring the officer's suggestion, Dylan got out of the car and I followed him. "What about if I stand here near to the sidewalk?" Dylan countered.

"That's fine. But stay back. Officer Towson and I will handle things from here."

I stood alongside of Dylan while both officers walked up to his mother's house. My heart raced at the speed of lightning. I was having so many different thoughts run through my head I couldn't think clearly. I've come to this house with Nick and Dylan, and we've never been able to get Bruce to open that front door. Hopefully, the officers will intimidate him enough that he will either let us see Mrs. Daisy or tell us exactly where she and Sonya are. "Think he's gonna answer the door?" I asked Dylan while Officer Vass was ringing the doorbell.

"I guess we'll see," Dylan replied.

While Officer Vass rang the doorbell we also witnessed him knock on the door. I wasn't counting but it seemed like he knocked and rang the doorbell at least eight times. "Looks like that bastard ain't opening the door," Dylan stated.

I sighed. "I guess you're right," I commented when I saw

both officers turn around to exit the porch. When they reached the driveway, surprisingly Bruce opened the front door. "Hey look, he opened the door," I yelled, trying to get the officers' attention.

"Yeah, he's standing in the door," Dylan yelled.

Both officers turned around and saw Bruce standing on the other side of the glass storm door, so they walked back onto the porch to approach him. "Think he's gonna let them in?" I asked Dylan.

"I don't even wanna think about it."

"I wonder what they are saying to him."

"Yeah, and I'm wondering what kind of lies he's telling them," Dylan spoke up.

"We'll soon find out," I said while I watched Bruce's body language from the other side of the glass door. He looked like he was playing it cool, like he was in control. That wasn't a good sign for Dylan and me. The goal was to get the officers to scare him, not let him control the situation.

"Wait, is he coming outside?" Dylan wondered aloud.

"It looks that way," I stated while I watched Bruce push the storm door open. Two seconds later he stepped onto the porch and closed the storm door.

Dylan and I couldn't hear anything Bruce was saying and that frustrated him. "What the fuck is going on? What are they saying to him?" Dylan started getting impatient.

"Baby, calm down. They got him to step outside, so let's wait and see what happens," I managed to say.

"I understand all of that, but they are taking too damn long. I need to see my mother and my sister," he spat.

Before I could comment, Officer Towson left Officer Vass on the porch with Bruce while he strolled on towards Dylan and me. The moment he was within arm's reach Dylan popped the first question. "Does he know where my sister is?"

"He says he doesn't know. He says that he hasn't seen her in a couple of days," Officer Towson replied.

"Sir, he is lying," I interjected.

"Well, did he tell you where my mother was? Because it seems like every time we come by here, he says that she either just left or she's asleep."

"Sorry to say, he just gave us that same excuse," the officer said.

"Listen, Officer, he's gonna have to give me a better answer than that. And I'm not leaving here until he does. As a matter of fact, tell him to let us in the house so we can check things out for ourselves," Dylan suggested.

"I can only ask him because that is his property."

"That is not his house. That's my mother's house. My father put her in that house," Dylan snapped.

I grabbed Dylan by the arm. "Baby, please calm down."

Dylan started yelling. "Nah, fuck that! Bruce, you think we're stupid. What, you put your hands on my mama again and now you're trying to hide her so we can't see the bruises? And tell me, where is my sister? What, you got her tied up in the basement or something? Cause she ain't been to work in a week!"

"Sir, I'm gonna have to tell you to leave if you don't calm down and control yourself," Officer Towson warned Dylan.

"Dylan, please stop." I began to beg him, but my words fell on deaf ears. Dylan snatched his arm away from me and made a run for the front porch. He sprinted across the lawn and jumped on the porch, over all three steps that led up to the front door. Luckily for Bruce, Officer Vass saw him coming and ushered Bruce back into the house. "Where the fuck is my mother and my sister, Bruce? Tell me where they at?" Dylan roared.

I finally made my way up to the porch, hoping I could help

defuse the situation before the officers hauled Dylan off to jail. "Sir, we're gonna ask you to leave the property. Now if you don't, we're gonna have to arrest you," Officer Towson warned him.

I reached for the back of Dylan's shirt and tugged on it. "Baby, come on, let's go."

"Bruce, answer my question. Where's my sister and my mama!" Dylan panted.

"You better listen to her," Officer Towson told him.

Dylan turned towards me and started making his way back down off the porch. But before he stepped off the last step, he looked back at the door while Bruce was standing there and said, "If I find out that you did something to my family, I'm telling you right now you better leave town ASAP."

"Come on, baby," I said once again, tugging on his shirt with a little more force. Thank God, this time he listened.

After Dylan and I climbed back into his car, both officers and Bruce kept their eyes on us as Dylan drove away. "Did you see how Bruce manipulated that whole situation?" Dylan roared. "He sure did because the main reason we had them follow us over there was so that he could tell us where Sonya is, since he said she was with my mama just yesterday. Now all of a sudden he doesn't know shit."

"So, what are we going to do now?" I wanted to know.

"I'm gonna get you to drop me off at Nick's spot. I'll get him to bring me home later."

"So, what's the plan?"

"The less you know, the better off you'll be . . ." Dylan said and then he fell silent.

"Dylan, please don't go back over to your mother's house."

"Listen, I don't care what no one says, I'm gonna find my mother and sister tonight."

I refused to dignify that statement with a comment. Right now, Dylan was in his feelings, so I left well enough alone.

It took Dylan approximately eighteen minutes to get to Nick's apartment. He pulled up to the apartment building, kissed me on the mouth, and then he hopped out of the car. I wanted to say something to him about the way he was carrying on, but I didn't. Instead, I crawled over into the driver seat, put the car in drive, and then I sped off.

I don't know how I got home without having a nervous breakdown, but I thank God that I didn't. Upon entering the parking garage, I couldn't hold the tears back. After I parked Dylan's car in the designated parking space, I sat there in the driver's seat and starting sobbing uncontrollably. I couldn't stop thinking about how things would be different if I hadn't gotten involved with Kendrick. My father wouldn't be dead, my former co-worker Nancy wouldn't be dead, or the Mahoneys. And who knows, maybe Kendrick had something to do with Sonya's disappearance. It's too much of a coincidence that no one had seen Sonya in over a week. But then when I thought about getting that text message from her a few days ago, I couldn't but wonder—was that her? Whatever the case, she was gone and we needed to find her.

Chapter 39

We're Fucked!

I sat in Dylan's car and sobbed for almost an hour. I finally willed my way out of the car after one of my neighbors saw me crying and offered to walk me to my apartment. After I accepted his hospitality, I allowed him to do just that.

As soon as I entered my apartment, I drank a glass of water and then I lay down on the living room sofa. I can't tell you how long I had been asleep, but I can tell you that when I woke up and saw that it was ten p.m., I became worried because there was no evidence that Dylan had come home while I was asleep, and when I tried to get him on the phone, he didn't answer it. In my mind, this wasn't good. Replaying the threats he made about killing Bruce kept playing over and over in my head. I just hoped that he hadn't gone through with it.

After ten minutes passed, I picked up my cell phone and tried his cell phone number again. But I got no answer. So, that's when I dialed Nick's number because I knew they were together. Unfortunately, Nick didn't answer his phone either. His voicemail picked up on the second ring. "Fuck!" I screeched and then I threw my phone down on the sofa.

I knew I wasn't going to be able to sit in the apartment and wait for Dylan to come home, so I grabbed my purse and my car keys and headed towards the front door. I said a silent prayer—*God, please be with me*—and then I opened the front door. "Fuck!" I blurted out, after opening my door and seeing Detective Grimes standing in the entryway with the same police officers that followed Dylan and me to Mrs. Daisy's house earlier. I knew something was about to go awfully wrong. I braced myself for the inevitable.

"Did we scare you?" Detective Grimes asked me while his partner and the two officers stood alongside of him.

I looked at his partner and the other two officers, then I looked back at him. "What do y'all want now? Aren't y'all tired of harassing me?" I asked him. I wasn't in the mood to deal with his shenanigans. I had other pressing matters on my mind that needed to be dealt with.

"We came to see if Dylan was home," he said.

"What do you want with him? Wasn't his case dismissed a couple of days ago?" I spat.

Before Detective Grimes could answer, Dylan came strolling down the hallway. Detective Brady saw him first. He nudged Detective Grimes to get his attention. "Mr. Callender, your timing is impeccable," Detective Grimes commented after he looked in the direction Detective Brady pointed.

I peeped my head around the doorway and when I saw Dylan's face, I knew he wasn't too happy to see all these cops standing at our front door. "Man, what the fuck y'all want now?" he roared.

Detective Brady spoke. "We just need to ask you a few questions."

"I see you got the two officers with you that kept me from going upside my mother's husband's head earlier today," Dylan hissed. By this time, Dylan was standing next to me in the doorway like he was ready to go toe-to-toe with these cops.

"Can we come in?" Detective Grimes asked boldly.

"Fuck nah! Are y'all motherfuckers crazy?" Dylan snapped.

218 / KIKI SWINSON

"Look, just tell us why y'all came here?" I interjected.

Detective Grimes looked at me and then he turned towards Dylan. "We came by to let you know that we found your mother's and sister's bodies."

Hearing the words *we found your mother's and sister's bodies* hit me in the chest like a ton of bricks. It hit Dylan even harder. I grabbed him by the arm and instantly felt him stiffing up. "What do you mean when you say bodies?" Dylan needed clarity.

"They're both deceased." Officer Towson spoke up. He was the same officer from earlier that talked to us while his partner, Officer Vass, talked to Bruce on the front porch.

"There's gotta be some kind of mistake. There's no way that my mama and my sister is dead," Dylan replied.

"How do you know that it's them?" I asked.

"They both had their identification cards on their persons," Detective Grimes stated.

"Where did you find their bodies?" Dylan wanted to know as his voice started cracking.

"In a storage unit that your mother's husband rented two weeks ago. And based on the level of the decomposition to their bodies, that was also around the time they were murdered," Detective Grimes replied.

"Oh my God!" I said, feeling completely horrified.

"So, that motherfucker killed my family?" Dylan roared as he broke away from my grip.

"We can't answer that question right now. But we are investigating all of the evidence fully," Detective Brady explained.

"Come on now, with that bullshit! You know that asshole murdered my family," Dylan huffed. "And where is he anyway? Did y'all arrest him yet?" Dylan's questions continued. He stood toe-to-toe with Detective Grimes and the other cops. Dylan's demeanor was stern, so they knew that he was serious.

"I'm sorry, but he's dead too." Officer Vass finally spoke.

"What the fuck do you mean, he's dead?" Dylan challenged Officer Vass.

"After we found your mother and your sister, we went by the house to serve him with a search warrant, and immediately after we entered the home, we found him lying on the floor of your mother's bedroom in a pool of his blood. It appeared that he shot himself in the head, but we can't be too sure. The gun that was used was a few feet away from his body," Grimes continued, as he looked at Dylan and me.

"Why the hell are you looking at us like that?"

"Because we're not ruling his death as a suicide. I have two officers here that heard you threaten to kill your mother's husband several times," Grimed said in a matter-of-fact kind of way.

"Oh, so now y'all wanna pin his death on me?" Dylan replied sarcastically.

"Only time will tell. But right now, we're gonna need the both of you to come down to the station so we can get a formal statement from you."

"I'm calling my lawyer before I go anywhere with y'all," I told them.

"By all means," Detective Grimes insisted as he stood there in the doorway.

I walked away from my front door to retrieve my purse and my cell phone. It was close to eleven p.m. and these assholes wanted to fuck with Dylan and me. I couldn't believe that Dylan and I were faced with yet another fucking murder investigation. When was all of this shit going to end?

Don't miss any of Kiki's thrilling novels

Available now from Dafina books

Read the original Wifey series

And

Check out the newest installments in Yoshi Lomax's story

PLAYING WITH FIRE

And

PLAYING THEIR GAMES

Available anywhere books are sold

WITHDRAWN

31901068815465